Everyone went into the room but Nate. He hung back.

Kinley shook her head. "What are you doing here?"

"I'm the big brother of the groom. He asked me to come, so I did," Nate said. "This is why I wanted us to chat earlier. Just to clear the air. Like I said, I was a jerk, and I'm sorry. I don't want anything to mess up Hunter's wedding."

Oh.

When he said it like that, he sounded so reasonable. And she realized that coming to Cole's Hill had more consequences than she'd thought. She was losing her professional edge because of Nate. Part of it was the way he made her pulse speed up. A bigger part was the fact that he was her daughter's father and she hadn't told him. And the cost of keeping that secret seemed higher than she might be able to pay.

"Sorry. I'm just a little short-tempered today. Must be the jet lag."

"Don't be. It happens to the best of us. After the tasting, can we get a drink and talk? It's obvious we're going to need to."

* * *

Tycoon Cowboy's Baby Surprise is part of The Wild Caruthers Bachelors duet:

These Lone Star heartbreakers' single days are numbered...

Dear Reader,

I'm so excited about the first book in my Wild Caruthers Bachelors series. You met the first Caruthers in *His Seduction Game Plan*. Hunter Caruthers is back and getting married in his hometown of Cole's Hill, a fictional town that incorporates my favorite parts of the Texas Hill Country. It is also the setting for *Pushing the Limits*, Space Cowboys #2.

Going home is never easy and for Kinley Quentin it's a little tougher than for most. The boy she had a crush on growing up—Nate Caruthers, the son of her father's employer—hooked up with her in Vegas two years earlier. And it was a fun weekend; the adult culmination of her teenage dreams, which was great until Nate went home and Kinley realized she was pregnant. She tried to get in touch and share the news with him but Nate wasn't ready to hear it. He was busy taking over running the Rockin' C Ranch and Industries, which is a full-time job. He didn't have time for a relationship with Kinley even though forgetting her was hard. He made a clean break...or so he thought.

Now she's back in town to plan Hunter's wedding and the past two years have given her an edge of sophistication, maturity and confidence she hadn't had in Vegas. She's hotter than before and Nate realizes he might have made a mistake when he said goodbye to her. But she has a daughter and that's a complication he isn't ready to deal with, especially when he learns the daughter is his.

Happy Reading!

Katherine

KATHERINE GARBERA

TYCOON COWBOY'S
BABY SURPRISE

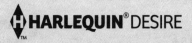

Recycling programs
for this product may
not exist in your area.

ISBN-13: 978-0-373-83847-9

Tycoon Cowboy's Baby Surprise

Copyright © 2017 by Katherine Garbera

Printed in U.S.A.

www.Harlequin.com

A12006 915993

USA TODAY bestselling author **Katherine Garbera** is a two-time Maggie Award winner who has written more than seventy books. A Florida native who grew up to travel the globe, Katherine now makes her home in the Midlands of the UK with her husband and a very spoiled miniature dachshund. Visit Katherine on the web at katherinegarbera.com, or catch up with her on Facebook and Twitter.

Books by Katherine Garbera

Harlequin Desire

Miami Nights

Taming the VIP Playboy
Seducing His Opposition
Reunited...With Child

Baby Business

His Instant Heir
Bound by a Child
For Her Son's Sake

Sons of Privilege

The Greek Tycoon's Secret Heir
The Wealthy Frenchman's Proposition
The Spanish Aristocrat's Woman
His Baby Agenda
His Seduction Game Plan

The Wild Caruthers Bachelors

Tycoon Cowboy's Baby Surprise

Visit her Author Profile page at Harlequin.com, or katherinegarbera.com, for more titles.

To Courtney and Lucas, who showed me that being a mom is about the best damned job any woman can have and for making my life so much richer.

As always special thanks to Charles for being a wonderful editor and for getting me. Also thanks to Nancy Robards Thompson, who originally brainstormed a version of this story with me.

One

"Pack your bags, kid, we're taking the show on the road," Jacs Veerling said as she swept into Kinley Quinten's office. The term was a stretch for the large workroom she shared with Willa Miller, the other wedding planner who worked for Jacs.

Jacs had the smarts of Madeleine Albright, the figure of Sofia Vergara and the business savvy of Estée Lauder. She was fifty but looked forty and had made her career out of planning bespoke weddings that were talked about in the media for years, even after the couples had split up. She wore her short hair in a bob, and the color changed from season to season. As it was summer, Jacs had just changed her color to a platinum blond that made her artic-blue eyes pop.

"Who's going on the road? Both of us? All three of us?" Kinley asked. Based in the Chimera Hotel and Casino in Las Vegas, they did in-house weddings, but the bulk of their business came from destination weddings all over the world. Wherever their A-list clients wanted.

"Just you, Kin," Jacs said. "I've inked a deal to plan the wedding of reformed NFL bad boy Hunter Caruthers. It's taking place in your home state of Texas, and when I mentioned your name, he said he knew you. Slam dunk for us. I think that might be why he picked our company over one in Beverly Hills."

Caruthers.

At least it was Hunter and not his brother Nate. "I can't."

Willa abruptly ended her call with a client, saying she'd call back, and turned to Jacs, who gave Kinley one of her patented she-who-must-be-obeyed stares.

"What? I'm sure I heard that wrong."

Kinley took a deep breath and put her hands on her desk, noticing that her manicure had chipped on her middle finger. But really she couldn't help the panic rising inside her. She had no plans to return to Texas.

Ever.

"I can't. It's complicated and personal, so I really don't want to go into it, but please send Willa instead."

Jacs walked over and propped her hip on the edge of Kinley's desk, which was littered with bridal gown catalogs and photos of floral arrangements. "He asked for you. Personally. That's the only *personal* that matters to me. Will you die if you go to Texas?"

"No. Of course not." Kinley just didn't want to see Nate again. She didn't even want to see her dad again in person. She was content with their weekly Skype chats. That was enough for her and for her two-year-old daughter, Penny.

"Is it because of your baby?" Jacs asked.

She'd told Kinley when she started that even though Jacs had made the decision to never have children herself, she understood that being a mom was an important role. She was very understanding about Kinley's needs and had a generous child-care policy for their small office.

"Sort of. She has just really settled into the day care here at the casino. Is it just a weekend trip?"

"Uh, no. I said pack your bags. You're going to be out there for the duration. That means six months. I'm taking on two more clients in Texas—one is a Dallas Cowboy and the other plays basketball for

San Antonio. I think you'll have plenty to keep you busy."

"Where would I stay?" Kinley asked, realizing there was no way to get out of the trip.

"I've rented a house in a nice subdivision…something called the Five Families. What an odd name," Jacs said.

"Is there anything I can say that will make you change your mind?" Kinley finally asked.

"Not really," Jacs said. "The client wants you, and you really have no reason not to go, do you?"

Yes. Nate Caruthers. The man who'd rocked her world for one passion-filled weekend, fathered her child and then interrupted her when she called later with that important news, telling her what happened in Vegas needed to stay there. He was her new client's older brother and still lived on the family's ranch outside Cole's Hill. But she didn't want to tell Jacs any of that. And she wasn't prepared to lose her job over it.

The only thing that was vaguely reassuring was that Nate would be too busy running the Rockin' C Ranch to be all that involved in wedding planning.

Fingers crossed.

"No reason. When do I need to start?" Kinley asked.

"Monday. I'm having Lori take care of all the details. You'll fly out on Friday, so you have time to settle in over the weekend. I've even included your nanny in the travel plans. Keep me posted," Jacs said as she turned on her heel and walked out of the office.

Kinley glanced down at the framed picture of Penny on her desk and felt her stomach tighten. After that disastrous call to Nate, she'd vowed not to allow him to let Penny down the way her own father had let her down. She just hoped that promise would be easy to keep once she was back in Cole's Hill. All she had to do was avoid Nate. Surely she could handle that except in this town she knew it would be impossible.

Nate Caruthers was a little bit hungover as he pulled his F-150 into the five-minute parking outside the Cole's Hill First National Bank. He reached for his sunglasses as he downed the last of his Red Bull before getting out of the cab of his truck. His younger brother was back in town, and that had called for a celebration that had lasted until the wee hours of the morning.

He tried the door on the bank, but it was locked. He leaned against the brick wall and pulled his hat down over his eyes to wait the five minutes until it opened.

"Nate? Nate Caruthers?"

The voice was straight out of his past and one of

his hottest weekends ever. He pushed the Stetson he had tilted to cover his eyes back with his thumb and looked over.

Kinley Quinten.

He whistled.

She'd changed. *Again.* Wearing some kind of lacy-looking white dress that ended midthigh and left her arms bare, she looked sophisticated. Not like the party girl he'd spent that weekend with almost three years ago in Vegas. His gaze followed the curve of her legs, ending at a pair of impossibly high heels. She looked like she'd stepped out of one of his mom's Neiman Marcus catalogs.

There may have been five years between them but none of that had mattered since he'd seen her in Vegas. She'd been twenty-three and he'd been twenty-eight.

"Eyes up here, buddy," she said.

He straightened from the wall and gave her a slow grin that many women had told them would get him out of any tight spot as he walked toward her. "Sorry, ma'am. Wasn't expecting you to look so good."

"Is that supposed to be a compliment?" she asked, opening her large purse and pulling out a pair of dark sunglasses, which she immediately put on.

"How could it not be? I guess the men in California must be blind if you're not sure."

She crossed her arms under her breasts. "I live in Las Vegas."

"Really? Since when? I thought you were only there to celebrate graduating from college," he said. "You should let me buy you a coffee after I'm done at the bank and we can catch up."

"Catch up? I don't think so. I'm in town for business, Nate," she said. "Plus, I think we said all that needed saying two years ago."

The door next to him opened with a gush of cold air-conditioning, and Kinley gestured for him to go first, but he shook his head. "Ladies first."

She huffed and walked past him.

He watched her move, her hips swaying with each of her determined steps. She probably wouldn't appreciate his attention, but he noticed that Stewart, the bank manager, was watching her, too.

Nate got in line behind her to wait for the cashier.

"I'm sorry I was such a douche on the phone. Can we please have coffee?" he asked. His mom always said, "If you don't ask, you don't get," and he wanted Kinley. Or at least to spend a little more time flirting with her before he headed back to the ranch.

She sighed. "One coffee, and then that's it. Okay?"

"Why will that be it?" he asked. "Maybe you'll want to see me again."

He grinned at her, and she shook her head. "I won't have time. I'm here for business."

"What business?" he asked. "Are you working at the NASA facility out on the Bar T?"

"No. I'm a wedding planner. I'm here to plan Hunter's wedding," she said.

"Well, I'll be damned."

"Yes, you will be," she said. An emotion passed over her face but too quickly for him to interpret it.

The cashier signaled Kinley over, and Nate stood where he was and observed her. She'd changed more than just her wardrobe, he realized. There was a core of strength that he hadn't noticed in her when they'd spent the weekend together. Maybe that was because they'd both been focused on having fun.

She concluded her business, and Nate stepped up to do his. He talked with Maggie, the cashier who'd been working the opening shift since before Nate had been born. When he was done, he looked around and noticed that Kinley was waiting for him by the exit.

She had her smartphone in her hand and was tapping out a message to someone. She'd pushed her sunglasses up on her head and was concentrating as she typed. She looked so serious.

He wondered what had happened in her life in the last three years and then realized he really had no right to find out. He'd ended their affair because her dad worked for his family and Nate wasn't really big on monogamy or commitment.

But seeing her again reminded him of how good that weekend had been and how hard it had been to hang up on her when she'd called and said she wanted to see him again.

She glanced up as he approached her.

"I hate to do this, but I can't make coffee this morning. I have to get my office set up here, and my boss has a potential couple scheduled for 10:00 a.m."

"Rain check, then?" he asked.

"Yes, that would be great," she said. She held her hand out to him.

She wanted to shake hands. Did she think this was a business deal? He took her hand, noticing how smooth and small it was in his big rough rancher hand. He rubbed his thumb over the back of her knuckles and then lifted her hand to his mouth to drop a kiss there.

"I'll be in touch," he said, turning and walking out of the bank. He went to his truck and realized his hangover was gone.

Kinley put Nate out of her mind as she unpacked the office and got the client meeting room set up. She glanced at her watch as she worked. The day care she'd signed Penny up for was two blocks down. Kinley wanted to get the room ready for the meeting with the basketball player and his fiancée and then go to see Penny before the meeting.

Her thoughts drifted back to Nate.

Damn.

He'd surprised her. Though she'd known she would run into him, she hadn't been prepared for it to be today. She'd sort of hoped to establish herself here first. She stood in the doorway and looked at the table she'd set up with a variety of faux cakes and flower arrangements.

Her phone rang and she glanced down. It was Jacs on the Skype app. She answered the call.

"Do you hate me now that you're back there?" Jacs asked.

"No. I don't hate you. But I could have used a little more time before seeing the client this morning," Kinley said.

"Sorry about the rush, kid, but these two are hot to get married. They want to expedite the timeline but still make sure everything is one of a kind. You are going to have to really work your contacts to get this done. But I have confidence in you. Also don't let Bridezilla bully you. She was full on this morning with me."

"I won't," Kinley said. Actually, it would be good to get straight to work. "I'm seeing the local baker this afternoon for the Caruthers-Gainer wedding. If she doesn't work, I'm going to see if I can get Carine to fly in from LA."

"Good. Do you need anything from the office here?" Jacs asked.

"I might after I talk to my ten o'clock. We still have the dress from the O'Neill-Peterson cancellation. She was very demanding. Maybe it will work for this bride if she doesn't know it was designed for another woman," Kinley said.

"I like your thinking. I'll have Lori email the sketches so you can use them," Jacs said. "Have a good one."

Jacs disconnected the call, and Kinley gave the room a final once-over. She nibbled on her bottom lip as she realized that she was rubbing the back of her right hand...the hand Nate had kissed.

She shook her head. This was a horrible idea. For one thing, she'd never really gotten over him. She hadn't been pining over him; she was too sensible for that, or at least that's what she told herself. But she still thought about him.

Still remembered all the things that had gone on in that big king-size bed in the Vegas penthouse suite. Sometimes she woke up in a sweat thinking about Nate.

Usually it only took a moment to shove those thoughts away. She'd been telling herself that he wasn't as good-looking as she'd remembered, but the way those faded jeans had hugged his butt this morning had confirmed he was.

And the spark of awareness that had gone through her, awakening desires that had been dormant since she'd given birth to her daughter, couldn't be ignored. Maybe it was like Willa had suggested to her last month. It was time to start dating again.

Yes, that was it. She'd find a nice guy, a townie, and ask him out for a drink. Or maybe she'd go to the local bar and see if she could find someone…to do what? She wasn't the party girl she'd once been.

She was a mom, and frankly the idea of going out and hooking up sounded like too much work—and not the kind she wanted to do.

She left the office, grabbing her purse and keys on the way out and locking the door behind her. She needed to see Penny.

Her daughter grounded her and made her remember what was really important.

As she walked down the streets of the historic district, she took stock of how far she'd come. When her parents had divorced, Kinley was a tomboy, the daughter of a housekeeper for one of the wealthiest families in Cole's Hill. Now she was living in one of the houses her mom used to clean and planning a wedding for the son of her father's boss. She felt like she'd come a long way.

Not that there had been anything wrong with her parents' careers, but she was different. She always had been.

She entered the day care facility and was shown to the room where Penny and the other two-year-olds were playing. Her daughter was right in the middle of a group that was clustered around some easels. She walked over to her daughter and stopped next to her.

"Hi, Mama," she said, dropping her marker and turning to hug Kinley's legs.

"Hey, honey pie," Kinley said, stooping down to Penny's level. "What are you making?"

"A horsey. That boy said he has his own," Penny said.

Kinley tucked a strand of her daughter's straight red hair behind her ear and brushed a kiss on her forehead. "There are a lot ranches around here."

"Like Pop-Pop's?" she asked.

Penny had seen the ranch on the many video chats they'd had with her father. And the last time they'd talked, her dad had taken his tablet into the barn and shown her his horse. The toddler couldn't wait to visit her Pop-Pop and meet his horse.

"Just like that one. But Pop-Pop just manages the hands. It's not his ranch."

"I can't wait to see it," Penny said.

"We might not get to go out there," Kinley said. She didn't want to take Penny to the Rockin' C and chance her running into Nate. She had no plans to tell Nate about Penny; he'd made it clear a long time ago where his interest lay, and it wasn't with raising a family. "Pop-Pop is going to come to town and visit us."

"Okay," Penny said.

Kinley hoped that would be the last of Penny talking about going to the ranch. She visited with her daughter until snack time, and when it was over, Kinley left after giving Penny a hug and a kiss.

She got through her meeting. She'd talked the bride, Meredith, into looking at the sketches for the dress they'd already had made. Meredith liked the design but wanted a few changes. Kinley was still thinking about that as she drove over to the Bluebonnet Bakery to sample the cakes for the Caruthers wedding.

She saw a familiar pickup truck with the Rockin' C logo on it parked out front but told herself not to jump to conclusions. The Rockin' C probably had a lot of F-150 pickups. It was probably just Hunter.

But when she walked into the bakery, she found her gut had been right. Nate stood at the counter along with his middle brother, Ethan, Hunter and a woman who had to be Hunter's fiancée. Derek, the second-oldest Caruthers, was a surgeon and probably not available to sample cake.

"Hello, everyone," Kinley said.

She just had to be professional. She could do that.

"Hi, I'm Ferrin Gainer," the woman said, stepping over to her. "It's so nice to meet you."

"I'm looking forward to working with you and helping you plan your special day. I've arranged for us to have a tasting in the back room," Kinley said, motioning everyone in the right direction. "Why don't you go through there and I'll be right with you."

Everyone went into the room but Nate. He hung back.

She shook her head.

"What are you doing here?"

"I'm the big brother of the groom. He asked me to come, so I did," Nate said. "This is why I wanted us to chat earlier. Just clear the air. Like I said, I was a jerk, and I'm sorry. I don't want anything to mess up Hunter's wedding."

Oh.

When he said it like that, he sounded so reasonable. And she realized that coming to Cole's Hill had more consequences than she'd thought. She was losing her professional edge because of Nate. Part of it was the way he made her pulse speed up; another, bigger part was the fact that he was her daughter's father and she hadn't told him. And the cost of keeping that secret seemed higher than she might be able to pay.

"Sorry. I'm just a little short-tempered today.

Must be the jet lag." Though with only a one-hour time difference between here and Vegas, she knew jet lag was a bit of an exaggeration.

"Don't be. It happens to the best of us. After the tasting we can get a drink and talk. It's obvious we're going to need to."

She nodded. She had to check in with her nanny, Pippa, and make sure that Penny would be fine for the evening. "I have one more appointment, and then I can meet you for a drink."

It would have been so much easier to just say no if Nate wasn't...well, so likeable and charming. And if she didn't have Penny. But she did. And now she was going to have make a decision that she'd thought she'd already made.

Two

Cake tasting. There were times when Nate wondered what had happened to his family. Though he didn't begrudge Hunter his happiness or his wedding, Nate liked things the way they'd always been: when the Caruthers were out working hard, playing even harder and making respectable mamas lock up their daughters.

"What do you think?" Hunter asked, pulling Nate aside so that they could speak privately for a moment.

"About what?"

"The cake. Do you have a preference?" he asked.

Nate shook his head. "I do like the idea of your groom's cake being shaped like a football field."

"That was discussed fifteen minutes ago. Where is your head?"

He looked over at the pretty redhead taking them through the different types of jam and icing that could be used between layers. Kinley. She was too much in his head. Going for a drink had *stupid* written all over it, but he'd never been one to back down from anything, even when it went against his own better sense.

"Don't do it," Hunter said.

"Don't do what?" Nate asked. Though he knew what his brother was talking about.

"She's practically family," Hunter said. "Marcus is like a second dad to us. Don't mess with her."

Too late. Nate recalled every detail of the weekend that he and Kinley had spent together; a part of him didn't want to ever forget it. Another part didn't believe it could have been as good as he remembered. But he knew it was. Then he remembered that silly little handshake she'd limited him to this morning at the bank and the rush of energy that had gone through them when they'd touched.

"I'm just looking."

"Make sure that's all you do," Hunter said.

He clipped his brother on the shoulder with his fist. "I don't take orders from you."

"You do now. Ferrin really wants this wedding

to be special. And that means not letting you, Ethan or Derek screw anything up. So be good."

"When have any of us ever been good?" Nate asked. He wasn't going to mess up Hunter's wedding. As much as he was against marriage himself, he really liked Ferrin and thought she was perfect for his brother. Hunter hadn't enjoyed being single the way the rest of the Carutherses did. His college girlfriend had been murdered and suspicion had fallen on Hunter for a good ten years before the real murderer had been convicted. So the only women Hunter had dated were those looking for a thrill… until Ferrin came along.

"I won't do anything to hurt your wedding," Nate promised.

Hunter reached over and squeezed his shoulder. "I know you won't. You've always looked out for me."

"Someone had to," Nate said. He loved his brothers and had always been the one to stand up for them.

"You two done over there?" their mother asked.

"Yes, ma'am. I was just saying how much I liked the mandarin filling," Nate said, luckily recalling the last cake he'd tasted.

"That's the one I am leaning toward as well," Ferrin said.

"Honey, that's my favorite, too," Hunter said, giving his fiancée the sweetest, sappiest smile Nate had ever seen. What the hell had happened to his brother?

"Then it's decided," Kinley said. "I have your other preferences marked down. Are you happy with this bakery? We can have one of our specialty bakers from Beverly Hills fly in and talk to you as well."

"We'd like to keep it local as much as we can," Ferrin said. "Hunter and I want this to be as authentic as it can be."

Kinley made some notes in her notebook, her hand gliding across the page. Nate couldn't help remembering the tomboy she'd been and the time he'd caught her sitting under one of the scrub oaks out in the pasture crying because her teacher said she had the worst handwriting in the class.

He shook his head. Where had that old memory come from? He had spent hours under that tree showing her how to write until her handwriting had been passable. It wasn't that he'd had the greatest handwriting, but Nate had never liked to be second best at anything. So he'd practiced a lot, and he remembered how grateful little Kinley had been that he'd helped her.

The women had moved to leave the room, but Ethan and Hunter hung back. Hunter just shook his head, but Nate noticed that Ethan watched until Kinley had rounded the corner.

"Dang. That Kinley sure has changed," Ethan said. "She makes a man—"

"Don't. She doesn't make you anything, Eth."

Both of his brothers turned to stare at him, and Nate knew he'd showed his hand without meaning to. But he wanted her. She had been his once and he knew himself well enough to know that he was going to try to make her his again. He didn't think it would last longer than it took her to plan Hunter's wedding, but damned if he was going to let any other man—especially one of his brothers—make a play for her.

"The lady might have something to say about that," Ethan said.

Nate shrugged. "We're having drinks tonight."

Ethan put his hands up. "Fair enough. I was just saying she sure isn't the girl who used to follow us around on horseback."

"No, she isn't," Nate agreed. He thought of all the changes he'd seen in Kinley and how much he appreciated each one of them. She'd been a party girl once, but she'd matured past that and he could see that she was stronger now. She'd changed and he acknowledged that he hadn't really, but one thing he knew for sure was that he still wanted her. And he was pretty sure they weren't finished with each other yet.

There had been something in her eyes when he'd shaken her hand earlier, maybe attraction, maybe something more. Whatever it was, he was hungry to explore it.

Ferrin was a marked contrast to the bride Kinley had been working with that very morning. They were in the office at the bakery discussing a few details. Where a true bridezilla would never take any of the first things that Kinley offered, Ferrin pretty much did. Her mom was a professor at UT Austin and wasn't able to make the cake tasting, so Ferrin did ask if Kinley would mind very much if they waited to finalize the cakes until her mom drove over on Saturday to give her opinion.

That was a very easy yes. Food was easy, Kinley thought, or it should be most of the time. It was a little bit funny to see all of the Caruthers brothers sitting around trying cake and pretending they cared what it tasted like, because even Ma Caruthers—as she'd always insisted Kinley call her—knew her boys weren't interested in cake flavors. They were here because Ferrin had asked Hunter to give his opinion and had suggested his brothers might want a say as well.

It was sweet.

The bond between the Carutherses was one of the many things that Kinley had always envied about them. Being an only child hadn't been a burden, but it had been lonely. Her parents both had demanding jobs that kept them away from home most of the time. She'd spent a lot of her childhood alone or tagging after the Carutherses. Now she was planning a wedding for Hunter… It was almost too much to be believed.

She made a few more notes. "Ferrin, what's your schedule like for the rest of the week? I'd love to get your dress selected. I have some designers that I like to use who are in New York and Beverly Hills, but also I have a friend from London who is just starting out. Her dresses are exquisite and I think they would flatter you."

"I'm teaching at Cole's Hill Community College on Thursday and Friday morning. But I'm free in the afternoon," Ferrin said.

"That's fine," Kinley said. "I can forward you the look books so you can go through the sketches and photos before you start narrowing down your choices."

Hunter came in as they were talking, and Kinley was very aware that Ethan and Nate were right behind him. She wasn't sure what they had been discussing, but given the way all three men stared at her…she guessed she'd been the topic.

"Hunter, y'all are free to go. We are going to be discussing the dress, and I want to surprise you on the big day," Ferrin said.

"Sounds good to me," Hunter said, coming over and giving her a kiss before leaving the room with his brothers behind him.

"Do you want my opinion?" Ma Caruthers asked. "I know you have your mother and you might want to make the decision with her."

"I'd love your opinion," Ferrin said, then turned to Kinley. "Tell me more about what will happen after I look at the designs in the books. Pretty much my entire bridal experience has been limited to episodes of *Say Yes to the Dress*. And I don't know how much of that is real or not."

"Well, once we have an idea of the type of dress you want, I'll get samples in similar styles shipped to us and then we'll arrange for you to try on all the different dresses until you narrow it down to a designer or a type of dress you like. Then someone from the designer you've chosen will be assigned to you to come out here and fit and measure the dress properly," Kinley said. Finding the perfect dress was really Kinley's favorite part of the wedding planning service. She was naturally organized, so the other parts of her job were easy and almost routine. Every wedding had food and cake and wine and music. But it was the dress and the theme that the bride selected that set each wedding apart.

"That sounds…exhausting," Ferrin said. "Also a little daunting."

Kinley walked over to the bride-to-be, who was a few years older than she, and put her arm around her shoulders. "Don't worry about anything. I will be by your side the entire time and we are going to plan the wedding of your dreams."

Ferrin turned and hugged her, and for the first time since she'd gotten off the plane in Texas, Kinley was glad she was here. Ferrin was the kind of bride that made her glad she was a wedding planner.

"Thank you."

"Told you you'd be in good hands with this one," Ma Caruthers said. "She's always had a good head on her shoulders."

"You've been wonderful to help me so much. I really appreciate it," Ferrin said to her future mother-in-law.

"Well, I never had any daughters and am hoping that you are going to give me a granddaughter one day. Thank you for letting me help out," Ma Caruthers said.

Kinley felt the heat in her chest and cheeks as she blushed. She hadn't considered anyone besides herself and Nate when she'd made the decision to keep Penny a secret from him. He was wild and not ready to settle down—she wasn't sure he ever would be—but his mother and father…they were nice people. People who wanted a grandchild.

And they already had one.

Kinley excused herself and left the bakery. Guilt weighed heavy on her shoulders as she walked to her car. It was hot on this summer afternoon, and she wished she could blame the heat for the feeling in the pit of her stomach. But she knew the truth. She'd let the secret of Penny go on for too long. There was no way to casually introduce her daughter to the Carutherses without them getting angry—justifiably so. She realized she might have bitten off more than she could chew by agreeing to come to Cole's Hill.

Now she was stuck between a rock and a very hard place. She could either stay here and hope that no one noticed Penny and that the guilt that had started to grow inside her would be bearable, or she could quit her job and run away from life.

She knew which option she wanted to choose. But she'd never been a coward, and she didn't want Penny to grow up thinking that she could run away from her problems. Kinley was going to have to figure out how to tell Nate he had a daughter, and she knew the sooner she did it the better it would be for everyone.

Nate had half expected Kinley to cancel on him and had gone to the Bull Pit with Ethan to have a drink while he was waiting for her to finish up with her afternoon appointments. What was it about Kinley that always made him feel on edge? With most of the women he dated he usually fell into a comfortable feeling pretty quickly. He knew what they liked and how to give it to them.

But not with her.

"Dad wants me to go to San Angelo to check on one of our mineral contracts. It's set to renew, and he's not sure if we should renew it or sell it," Ethan said. He was the family lawyer but also worked for a big-time law firm. He used to work in Houston but now handled his clients from his home office here in Cole's Hill. "Then I'm probably going to fly to LA and be back a few days later."

Ethan had a woman in Los Angeles. They all knew it but he never mentioned her, so Nate had figured she was either casual or married. And since he didn't want his brothers nipping in his own business, he'd never asked.

"Sure thing. We aren't doing anything major this week. Mitzi is looking for men for the Fourth of July bachelor auction… She's suckered a few of those astronauts into doing it and has a theme of American Hero for this year's event. She wanted Hunter, but since he's off the market he promised to get a friend from Dallas."

"Then why does she need me?" Ethan asked.

"Well, we all know lawyers are sharks, so it must be that she remembers your gold buckle rodeo days and wants to have you as a cowboy in the lineup." Nate liked to rib his brother about being a lawyer but he'd be welcome at the auction.

"How about I just make a large donation and sit on the sidelines?" Ethan said.

They all felt about the same way when it came to participating in events like the charity auction. "You can't. One of the Carutherses already did."

"Derek? He's a doctor—he should be used to this kind of thing," Ethan said.

"He is and he likes the attention, so he said yes as soon as she asked," Nate said.

"You?"

Nate shrugged. "I have been dating her off and on, so she was willing to let me out of it."

"Well, damn. Okay, I'll do it," Ethan said.

"Good," Nate said. He thought it would do his brother some good to find a woman here in Cole's Hill whom he liked instead of driving to Midland whenever he wanted to hook up. Or whatever Ethan did over there.

"So when's your date with Kinley?" Ethan asked as he took a swallow of his beer.

"We're having drinks tonight," Nate said.

"Drinks? That's not a date," Ethan said.

"Isn't it?"

"Hell, no. You and I are having drinks and this sure as hell isn't a date," Ethan said.

"Damned straight," Nate said. "I've never had any problems turning drinks into something more."

"None of us have," Ethan said. "Can you believe Hunter is getting married? I thought…well, I guess we all thought that he was never going to find a woman who'd trust him."

"I know," Nate said. He didn't like to think about how many times he'd defended his brother in places like the Bull Pit and in boardrooms whenever someone had brought up Hunter's past. Gossip had it that their family had bought Hunter's freedom, but the truth was the cops never had enough evidence to charge him with murder. Not that that had made any difference in the court of public opinion. "I'm glad to see him so happy. Damned if I could have ever seen any of us as married, but being engaged looks good on him."

"It does. Ferrin seems to be an important part of his new life. And I'm going to deny saying this if you bring it up, but he seems like a new man now."

Nate had to laugh at that. Hunter was a new man. A man freed from the past and the guilt that he'd carried for ten years.

"Guilt did weigh on him. That's why I lead a free and easy life. The only thing that weighs on me is the family business, and to be honest I like a good tussle in the boardroom, so that's not really a big deal."

Ethan laughed. "You said it, brother. Speaking of a business, Dylan Gallagher has a Cessna he wants to sell us. He's thinking of buying a big jet."

"What does he need a jet for?"

"Apparently, he has a lady friend on the East Coast he wants to visit," Ethan said. "I'll drive over and look at it this afternoon. It would be nice to have it as a backup for the older one we've been thinking of getting rid of."

"It would be. Ranch assets are your domain, so if you think we should buy it, I'll agree with you."

"Wish all things with you were this easy to settle," Ethan said.

Before Nate could respond, his phone beeped and he glanced down at the screen to see he had a text message from Kinley. Nate finished his beer and stood up. "I'm easy to get along with. You're the troublemaker."

Ethan's laughter followed him out the door. He left his pickup in the parking lot at the Bull Pit and walked across town to the restaurant where Kinley was waiting for him. The sun was setting as he came around the corner and he saw her standing to the left of the entrance. She was backlit by the sun, which silhouetted her curves and seemed to highlight her reddish-brown hair. He stopped for a minute as he realized that he didn't want to screw this up.

He'd hurt her with the way he'd behaved when she'd called him from Vegas, and this was a fresh start. The kind of thing that he needed with her, because no matter what he'd said to her on the phone, one weekend hadn't been enough to get her out of his system.

Three

Kinley had a rushed dinner with Penny and her nanny before leaving to meet Nate. Tonight was important, and she needed to be stronger than she'd ever been before. She'd dressed carefully, choosing a gray cap-sleeve dress that nipped in at the waist before ending at the knees. She'd paired it with a piece of costume jewelry she'd purchased at a vintage shop in Melrose the year before her mom had died.

Wearing it always made Kinley think of her mom. She touched it like a talisman, trying to glean a little of her mom's courage before Nate showed up. She was scared.

She'd made the only choice she felt she could make when she'd decided to have Penny and to raise her daughter on her own. But circumstances had changed, and it was time to make another choice.

She pulled her phone out of her purse for the tenth time since she'd texted Nate that she was waiting for him at the Peace Creek Steak House, not because she expected him to respond, but because she felt so vulnerable just standing there waiting for him.

She heard a group of people approaching the entrance and looked up to see Bianca Velasquez walking toward her. Her mom had cleaned the Velasquez home way back when, and Bianca and Kinley had been really good friends. She smiled when she noticed Kinley, waved her friends on and came over to give her a hug.

Her friend had thick black hair that she wore long and falling around her shoulders and olive skin Kinley had always envied. She was wearing a pair of slim-fitting white jeans and a flowy navy-colored blouse.

"I didn't know you were back in town," Bianca said.

"I didn't know you were, either. I thought you were still in Spain," Kinley said. Bianca's young husband had recently died in a fiery car crash, leaving the window with an eighteen-month-old son to raise. Kinley and Bianca kept in touch by email and had a lot to share since they both were single moms.

"I recently moved back. Mom and Dad were really persistent. And I missed Texas," Bianca said. "Do you have plans tonight? You can join us."

"I'm only back for a few months to plan Hunter's wedding," Kinley said. "I'm meeting someone but I'd love to catch up sometime."

"Me, too. I'm looking for a job, believe it or not," Bianca said in a sort of self-effacing tone. "I have your number, so I'll text you and we can find some time to meet up with our kiddos."

"Sounds great," Kinley said, hugging her friend and realizing how nice it was to see Bianca. The combination of secrets and guilt had been weighing on her, but seeing a friendly face, making some normal plans, made her feel better.

Bianca waved goodbye before going into the restaurant. Kinley felt someone watching her and glanced up to see Nate at the end of the driveway, walking toward her. He hadn't changed since their earlier meeting; he still wore dark jeans paired with what she knew was a designer shirt and hand-tooled, custom-made leather boots. He walked like a man who knew his place in the world. He was confident and sure, and a part of her truly resented him for it.

She'd been struggling to figure out her place her entire life. She might not have been aware of it when she'd been younger, but these days it felt like a yoke around her neck. Like she'd been carrying it for too long. Part of it, she knew, was the burden of what she had to tell him and her own uncertainty about how to do it, but she knew another part was the fact that she felt like she was always running to catch up.

Probably that could be traced back to living two different lives for most of her upbringing: the weeks in town with her mom at the Velasquez home and the weekends on the ranch with her father.

"Nate, I'm glad you could make it," Kinley said. To her own ears, her voice sounded too bright. Like she was trying to force out a happiness she didn't feel. But she put a smile on her face, determined to keep it in place until she actually could smile around him.

"It was my idea, so I wasn't about to say no." He winked at her as he reached her, putting his hand at the small of her back to turn her toward the entrance.

She moved forward, trying to ignore the pulsing that had started as soon as she felt his hand on the small of her back. His hands were big and hot and made her very aware of the last time he'd touched her there.

They'd both been naked and he'd rolled her onto her stomach in that big king-size bed to give her a massage, which had ended with him deep inside her as she'd climaxed again and again. A shiver of pure sexual need went through her.

It had been a long time since any man had touched her save for her ob-gyn, and Kinley, who had been too tired to think of dating before this, now thought that might have been a huge mistake.

She wished she'd had at least one other man since Nate so she'd have some sort of buffer. He reached around her to hold open the door, and she was both elated and disappointed that he broke contact.

She stepped inside, waiting a moment for her eyes to adjust to the dim interior. She was losing control of herself, which would mean loss of control of the situation if she didn't pull herself together.

She skimmed the bar and spotted a booth in the back that looked like it would give them some privacy from the other patrons in the steak house.

"I see a spot," Kinley said, walking toward it quickly, not giving Nate a chance to touch her back again.

Touching her had been a mistake, because as he watched her walk through the bar, images of the last time he'd touched her back ran through his mind. He remembered the afternoon sunlight shining into their room and how creamy her skin had looked against the white hotel sheets. She had freckles on her back, and he'd taken his time to touch and caress each of them before he made love to her.

A jolt of need went through him, and he knew whatever lie he'd been telling himself about meeting up with Kinley to clear the air was paper-thin. He wanted her. And pretending that there was anything other than that motivating him would be a mistake.

She slid into the booth she'd spotted in the corner. It was darker back here, lit only with an electric fixture mounted on the wall that was made to look like a gas lamp. The bulb flickered like a live flame. They had more privacy than he'd expected.

He started to slide in next to her, but she shook her head and gestured for him to sit across from her. He sat down on the hard wooden bench, hoping it would cool him down, but it didn't. Instead his legs brushed against hers under the table, and every time he inhaled all he could smell was her perfume. It was some kind of flowery, summery scent that made him more determined that they should spend the summer together.

He was a temporary guy and she was here temporarily; it should be easy enough for both of them. But his gut warned it wouldn't be. It couldn't be. First of all, her job was going to bring her into contact with his family—a lot. Second, her dad was his foreman, and Nate didn't want to do anything to compromise that relationship. Plus—and this was the big one—he was pretty sure that Kinley had already written him off.

So he was going to have to figure out how to convince her that he was more than a wealthy playboy. Was she worth it?

Even as he asked himself that question, he knew the answer was yes. There was something in her big chocolate-brown eyes that made him determined to figure out what he needed to say or do to claim her as his own.

"What are you drinking?" he asked. His voice sounded almost too loud in the quiet intimacy of the booth.

"Sparkling water with a twist of lime," she said.

"I can't order that at the bar or they will laugh me out of here," he said.

"Then I'll order it. What do you want?" she asked. He noticed that her tone was all business, and he realized that while he was thinking this was the first step to renewed intimacy, she wasn't.

"I was joking, Kin. I'll get the drinks," he said. "I'm ordering something to eat as well."

"Thank you," she said as he left the booth to go and place their order.

A good five minutes had passed before he returned to their table. He put the glasses down before retaking his seat.

"I'm sorry about overreacting about the drink. I'm a little on edge tonight," she said.

"Planning weddings is stressful work?" he asked. He took a swallow of his beer and leaned back, stretching one arm along the back of the wooden bench.

"Sometimes. Ferrin's such a sweetie, so she's making my job pretty easy. But I'm working with another client who is a bit more demanding," Kinley said.

"I never would have pictured you as a wedding planner," Nate said. When he'd known her as a child, she'd been so rough-and-tumble. The kind of cowgirl who could do anything the boys could on the ranch. His parents had always treated his brothers and him the same way they did all the kids whose families worked on the ranch. That meant they all did chores together and they all got a horse of their own to take care of. It was a tradition that Nate had followed when he took over running the ranch from his dad a few years ago.

The Caruthers fortune derived from the cattle they ran on their property as well as oil and mineral leases they'd had for generations and the newer stud operation that was just fifteen years old. The stud farm had been Kinley's dad's idea for diversifying the ranch.

"I guess you don't know me," she said. "I like planning weddings."

"You might be right that I don't know certain things about you," he said. "But I'd argue there are parts of you I know very well."

She flushed. Her skin was so creamy and pale that any time she was aroused, angry or embarrassed it flashed in a pinkish red across her face.

"Don't, Nate," she said. "Please do not bring up that weekend in Vegas or our intimacy again. I really would rather your brothers and parents didn't know about it."

He leaned forward over the table. "There isn't anyone here but you and me, Kin, and we both know what happened."

"We do. And we both remember how it ended... or is that just me?"

"I already apologized for that," he said, sitting back. Damned if it wasn't just like a woman to keep reminding him of how he'd screwed up.

"I know. And I accepted your apology. All I meant by my comment was that we're like oil and water—we don't mix very well."

He thought they'd mixed just fine. But arguing now would just get her back up more and not move them any closer to the ending he wanted for them. He knew he had to ease up, and he did. "I'm not the same man I was three years ago."

She gave him a small smile and nodded. Then she laced her fingers together, and he noticed she wore a small thin ring on her middle finger. "Fair enough. I'm definitely not the same woman. So what's changed with Nate Caruthers?"

Kinley knew she was stalling, but honestly she needed more time. She toyed with the lime on the side of her glass, rubbing it around the rim to distract her from the fact that Nate's big frame dominated the corner booth. His legs were on either side of hers, the rough fabric of the denim abrading the bare skin of her legs. She tried to shift but just ended up rubbing her leg against his.

She glanced over at him to see if he'd noticed. He had.

He didn't say anything. Instead he took a sip of his beer, and she watched the muscles of his throat work as he swallowed and then leaned back, stretching his legs out under the table, brushing them against hers again.

"I'm still doing some investment stuff, but my main focus now is running the ranch. Dad wanted to ease off on the everyday running of the Rockin' C. And as you know, it's a full-time job. So I stepped up," Nate said.

The Rockin' C was one of the largest ranches in Texas. They ran cattle, had oil, operated a stud farm and employed more than one hundred families on the property. They weren't gentleman farmers; they were more like the Ewings of TV's *Dallas*.

"Where are your folks living now?"

"Still on the property. Mom wanted a smaller house, so they built a five-bedroom ranch house out near the small lake."

"That's small?" she asked with a laugh.

"For her. Plus she said she wanted enough room to spoil her grandkids once we all settled down," Nate said.

Once again Kinley felt the white-hot needle of guilt pierce through her. "When is that going to happen?"

"Not any time soon, as far as I'm concerned. Hunter is the only one who seems interested in getting serious. But after ten years of hell, I think it's about time he had a break."

"That stuff about him… It was really hard to watch when I was in California. I mean, there was the Hunter I grew up with and then this other guy I was seeing stories about on TV. I'm glad they finally caught the man responsible."

"We all are. Mom spent a lot of time at St. Thomas Aquinas Church praying," Nate said.

When he spoke about Hunter, Kinley heard the love and concern in his voice. She'd been in high school when Hunter had first been accused of murder, but all that was in the past now. And Hunter had Ferrin.

"He's got the happy ending he deserved," Kinley said. It gave her hope that once she came clean with Nate she'd be able to move on. Maybe keeping Penny's paternity a secret was one of the barriers that had kept her from dating over the last few years.

But she knew it wasn't. She knew it was her own fear of trusting a man again. Or, to be more honest, trusting her heart. She'd thought what she felt for Nate had been the beginning of something more solid, but in the end it had only been lust.

Which was raising its hotter-than-hell head once again.

"He has. How many weddings have you planned?" Nate asked. "How did you get started doing that?"

She sipped her sparkling water and took the reprieve he'd unintentionally given her. "I've planned close to twenty weddings. All of them high-end, destination-type affairs. I got started when I answered an ad for a personal assistant and starting working for Jacs. She had one of her planners flake out and gave me a trial run. I guess she saw something in me and decided to promote me to planner."

"I'm not surprised she saw something in you. I've never known you to be a woman to back down," Nate said. "No matter how much the outer packaging has changed over the years, that solid core of steel still remains."

It was one of the nicest things that anyone had ever said to her. That Nate Caruthers was the one saying it made her heart heavy. "Thank you."

"It's okay. I should have remembered that when you called me. Instead I felt trapped, and I wasn't ready for that. Despite the fact that we spent a weekend together, you're not the kind of woman a man should ever be casual about."

She didn't know what to say to that. The fact that he hadn't been ready to settle down gave her pause in her determination to tell him about Penny. Was he ready now? How would she know for sure?

She wanted to make things right. For Nate. For Ma Caruthers. For herself. But her duty was to Penny. And Kinley had to determine if it would be better for her daughter to never know who her father was or to know and have him disappoint her.

It was a tough call.

One that was going to take more than a sparkling water and a single conversation to figure out. She wasn't sure if it was cowardice or not, but she decided she needed to get to know the man that Nate was today before she let him know he had a daughter.

It was the only fair thing to do for herself and Penny. And for Nate, who was still running wild, if word around town could be believed.

"I'm not sure that I was ready for anything more during that weekend in Vegas," she admitted. "But I am definitely not as casual now."

"Can I talk you into dinner?" he asked.

She hesitated, but she'd already said good night to Penny, so she knew her daughter wasn't expecting her home until after bedtime. Kinley had promised to call at seven thirty and could still do so.

If she was going to figure out how and if to tell Nate, they were going to have spend more time together, and dinner seemed like a safe enough way to start.

Four

Nate normally would have gone to the country club for a midweek dinner and then played a few games of pool with Derek before hitting the Bull Pit for more drinking and carousing before heading home. Instead he was seated across from Kinley eating a steak and listening to her talk about the latest book she'd read.

He didn't want to dwell on the fact that this was shaping up to be one of his best weeknights in a long time. She was animated when she talked, and now that he'd put the brakes on anything too sexy, she'd relaxed. Her hands moved as she explained a part of the book she really liked, and then she laughed and his gut clenched and his blood seemed to flow a little heavier in his veins.

"It's just the funniest thing I've read in a long time and I thought while I was reading it, *this girl could be me*. Have you ever felt that way?" she asked.

He hadn't. "Not really, but then, I've always had Dad to show me the kind of man I wanted to be."

"Your dad is the best," she said.

There was a note in her voice that made him wonder if Marcus hadn't been the same kind of dad as his was. His father lived for his sons and made sure they knew it. They'd all been very certain that he had a strong moral code for them to live up to and he expected a lot from them. But he'd always treated them with love.

"Was your dad?" Nate asked.

"He wasn't horrible or anything like that. But he did tend to work a lot on the weekend when I was out there. Mostly I think I saw your dad more than I saw my own."

Nate hadn't realized that and now wondered if he was keeping any of his employees from seeing their kids as often as they liked. He never really thought about the ranch children. His life was very different from his employees', since his days of working the ranch were long gone. He spent most of his time in his high-rise office building here in Cole's

Hill doing deals and managing the business that the Rockin' C had blossomed into.

"I didn't know that," he said, at last understanding that there was a lot to Kinley that he didn't know.

In his mind he always imagined that she'd had the same sort of upbringing he had. He remembered Kinley being on the ranch on the weekends. He'd thought of her as a sort of girl version of himself.

"Why would you?" she asked. "It would be weird if you had. Besides, my dad and I have a pretty good relationship now. It's just different than yours is with your parents."

Nate shook his head. "I was very glad to move them into their own home, not that I forced them out. But as much as I like having my town house in the Five Families area, I do prefer to be out on the ranch."

"Couldn't you have lived there with your parents?" she asked.

"Of course, but if I did, then Mom wanted to meet any of the women I brought home, and sometimes that could get awkward."

"I bet," she said. "Are you still mostly keeping it casual?"

"Mostly. But I am here with you tonight."

"Tonight? Should I just be thinking of this as temporary… What am I talking about? We're having dinner to clear the air and give us a friendly base so that we don't make Hunter and your family aware of what happened between us."

He should have been very happy that she understood the kind of man he was.

But…

He didn't want her to dismiss him so easily. Yeah, he was a temporary cowboy, the kind of man who knew how to show a woman a good time for a short stretch, but he might change for the right woman.

That was a big ask, though. And Kinley was perfectly within her rights to friend zone him the way she had.

"Fair enough. But for the record, you're not like everyone else," he said.

She paused for a second, her eyes widened, and he realized that a part of her wanted him to be Mr. Right. He could see it there in her gaze, and he'd never been anything close to that.

"Really?"

There was so much hope in her tone that it was almost painful to listen to it. He was afraid of hurting her and before this moment hadn't been aware of how likely it was that he could. He'd thought she was like him. The female version. Party girl to his party boy and that like him she'd segue into the next phase of her life as a successful businesswoman.

But in her eyes was a hope that he hadn't counted on or ever seen before.

She wanted him to be a hero.

Not a bad boy.

Could he do it? Could he be the man she wanted?

The selfish part of him wanted to pretend he hadn't noticed and maybe just go with it. But he had always prided himself on being honest in all of his relationships, and pretending was a form of lying. Some would say the worst form.

"Yes. You are very special," he said at last.

She fumbled for her water glass and took a sip before placing it carefully back on the table.

"You're kind of unforgettable, too," she said.

Just like that he knew he could have Kinley again if he wanted to. If he kept his mouth shut and acted the part. But he'd already decided that would be the kind of low-down behavior he wouldn't indulge in. But, oh, he was very tempted.

Her mouth was full and peach colored in the ambient lighting of the restaurant, and he was so tempted to just lean across the table and kiss her. To stop talking before he did anything that would ruin whatever it was she thought she saw in him.

Kinley was teetering on the edge. There had been a flash of something in Nate that made her want to believe he could be the kind of man who would spend the rest of his life with her. And though she was killing it—or at least managing it—as a single mom, there were times when she fantasized about having the perfect family that she'd always dreamed of having as a child. Growing up her family hadn't been perfect, and she'd believed when she finally had kids she'd do it the right way. Have that perfect family from television and magazine ads that she'd always craved.

And now Nate was here sitting across from her saying things about how she was different from other women and looking at her…like he might have changed in the last two years. But she couldn't just take a chance on that being the truth. She needed to be logical with this man whom she'd never been able to be logical about.

He'd always fascinated her. When she was younger, Nate had been the Caruthers who'd always looked out for her when she'd been on the ranch for the weekend. Then when she'd grown into her awkward preteen self, she had crushed on him—hard.

Now he tempted her again. Not with his easy charm and good looks, but with the slightest hint that he might be the partner she lacked. The father Penny needed.

She reached for her wineglass and took a sip. She was riding the crazy train straight to some sort of dreamlike existence that she knew didn't exist. She knew that Nate was a great guy, sexy as hell and able to make any woman feel like she was the center of his world. And there were times when Kinley was able to make herself believe that she had been the center of it for that weekend in Vegas. But then he'd moved on.

A new business interest caught his attention, probably a new woman and a new expensive toy. She had to keep her wits about her.

But she liked him.

She'd always liked him. And it had been a really long time since a man—any man—had looked at her the way Nate was now.

And she'd left herself the slightest bit vulnerable when she'd just gone with her gut and told him he was unforgettable. He was. Even if she hadn't had Penny to remind her of him every day, she doubted she would have been able to stop thinking about him.

"So...?" she said at last. Yeah, she was great at conversation, she thought. She could handle a full-on bridezilla on the warpath trying to make her special day the most fantastic ever, but put her across the table from this man and her verbal skills suddenly dropped to nothing.

"How do you feel about getting out of here and taking a walk around the plaza? The city commission is sponsoring a light show on the side of city hall that I've heard is pretty amazing," he said.

It sounded so nice and normal. Like a real date. Except, was this a date? She wasn't about to ask him and make herself look silly. But they'd said drinks, and now it had turned into dinner. She was holding a secret she needed to share and no closer to actually figuring out how to do it. And he had invited her to do something that sounded so normal.

So not a part of the chaos in her mind.

"I'd love to," she said. She glanced at her watch, realizing it was almost time for her to call Penny and say good-night. "I need to make a call first."

She reached for her wallet to leave some money toward the bill, but he stopped her. "I've got dinner. Go make your call. I'll meet you out front."

She got to her feet, put her purse over her shoulder and left the table. She glanced up and noticed that Bianca was watching her. Her friend waved. Kinley waved back, realizing how much she'd missed living in a town like Cole's Hill. These people were part of her past, and they knew her. She had a connection here that she'd never have in Vegas.

She'd missed it.

She wanted so much for Penny. Not just that perfect fantasy family in her mind, but also to have friends like Bianca, a solid base for her childhood so she'd always know where she came from.

She stepped outside, noting that the sky was clear and the sun was starting to set. She walked away from the entrance of the restaurant. At a safe distance, she hit the video call app on her phone and dialed Penny's iPad. Her daughter would be waiting for their good-night ritual.

"Mama!" Penny said as the call connected.

"How are you, sweet girl?" Kinley asked.

Her daughter was nestled into her pink cotton pajamas with her red ringlets fanning out behind her head as she lay propped up in the bed. She had her stuffed rabbit, Mr. Beans, tucked under her arm, and her eyes looked sleepy.

"Good. We just read the fishes," she said.

Which was what Penny called Dr. Seuss stories. All of them. Kinley had started reading her *One Fish, Two Fish* from the time she was tiny. And now anything that rhymed was *the fishes*. "Yay. Those are our favorites. Good night, sweet girl."

"Night, Mama."

"Love you."

"Love you, too," Penny said, waving her chubby little toddler hand at the screen. "Bye-bye."

Kinley waved back. "Bye-bye."

She disconnected the call and then held the phone to her chest for a long minute. She had never realized she could love anything as much as she loved her daughter, and she would do anything to protect her.

Never had the challenge of ensuring that been harder, she thought as she heard voices at the entrance and turned to see Nate talking to a group of three women. They were all Texas beauties with straight blond hair and charming accents, and Nate was being his usual flirty self with them.

Had whatever she thought she'd seen in his eyes just been her projecting what she wanted to see?

Most Texas towns prided themselves on their history, and Cole's Hill was no different. Unlike other towns that could trace their history back to the original Spanish land grants, Cole's Hill had been a dusty stop on cattle drives from Houston and little more for a long time. It had gotten steadily bigger in the 1800s and 1900s until it was one of the fastest-growing small towns in the United States by the early 2000s. Today it blended the broader Texas history with the local traditions that had helped build the community.

The five families who'd originally settled in Cole's Hill were still a big part of the town. Nate's family was one of them, and he served on the Cole's Hill Committee along with several other members of the Five Families. This summer's light display was just part of their yearlong heritage celebration.

Something had changed between the time Kinley had left the table and when he met up with her outside the restaurant. She was more subdued than before and seemed to have her barriers up. She wasn't as chatty as she'd been, and he noticed when she spoke she wasn't as animated.

"The light display is being put on by the local community college and high school multimedia programs. We asked them to take the history of the town and turn it into a show. I haven't had a chance to see it yet," Nate said as they walked into the town square.

"It sounds pretty interesting," she said. "How long is it running?"

"Every Friday, Saturday and Sunday evening during May, June and July," he said. "With the new space facility here we are getting a huge surge in population, and we want to make sure that we don't lose anything that makes Cole's Hill special."

He had no idea why he was talking about the town so much when what he wanted to do was tell her how pretty she looked tonight. But instead he was sticking to the safer topic.

At the end of the meal, he'd run into a few of the women he dated casually over the years, and it had made him aware of the fact that those women knew him pretty well and knew what to expect from him. Not one of them had ever looked at him the way

Kinley had at dinner—like he was more than just a good time. That look she'd given him was making him want to believe he could be more with her.

"I'm really glad to hear it. Is there a good spot to view it?" she asked.

City hall dominated one side of the square. Two more sides were lined with shops and restaurants. On the fourth side was a mixed-use luxury high-rise that had both offices and penthouse apartments, including his own. The square itself was dotted with trees and benches and a statue of Jake Cole, who had given the town its name. During the war of Texas independence, he'd made a stand here.

"I'm told that anywhere we can see the front face of city hall is good, but I have a special viewing area in mind," he said.

He'd texted his assistant, Ben, and asked him to set up the balcony for them to watch the light show. He put his hand on the small of Kinley's back again, this time spreading his fingers wider to touch more of her.

"Stop doing that."

"What?"

"Touching me. I don't need your hand to steady me," she said.

He dropped his hand, then lifted it up toward her shoulder. "My father raised me to be polite to ladies."

"Well, thank you. I appreciate that," she said. "Where is this spot that you think we should view it from?"

He pointed up to his balcony.

"From your apartment?" she asked.

"It really is a better view," he said. "And I thought we were friends. Surely if Bianca invited you to her place to watch the light show, you'd have no problem with that," he said.

She tipped her head to the side and studied him. She nibbled on her lower lip, which just made him want to groan, as it drew his attention to her kissable mouth. It was full and lush and it didn't matter to him what she said. He always wanted to feel it under his.

"Are you saying that you and Bianca are interchangeable?" she asked.

What? He wasn't even paying attention to anything other than the fact that there was a spark in her eyes as she teased him. Teasing him was a very good sign, and he knew he was one step closer to having her where he wanted her: in his apartment, where he could maybe convince her to give him another shot. Another chance.

"Not at all," he said. "Bianca is a lovely person, but she and I are very different."

He took a step closer to Kinley until barely an inch of space separated them and leaned in closer, giving in to the temptation that had been taunting him all evening. He brushed his lips across hers and felt a jolt go through his entire body. He pulled back, because they were in the square and crowds were starting to build. And what he wanted from Kinley was too private to be shared in public.

"I want something from you that I don't think Bianca does," he said, then put his hand on the small of Kinley's back again and turned her toward his building. She didn't flinch or pull away but just walked next to him.

Five

Kinley stopped thinking about everything and reminded herself she was twenty-six years old. Sometimes she felt ancient, but when Nate kissed her she felt a spark of the young woman she was and she wanted to run with it.

She smiled at several people who looked vaguely familiar as they walked past her. She had a feeling that Nate was her kryptonite, that he was the one man she'd never be able to resist.

She'd been right to have that jolt of fear when Jacs had first told her she was coming back to Cole's Hill. The completely crazy thing she was just now realizing was that her secret about Penny hadn't been the reason for her apprehension.

She knew it wasn't the smartest choice and that tomorrow she'd have to deal with that, but for right now there was a pulsing in her body and an empty ache that she wanted to fill. She walked slightly ahead of him on his left. His hand was like a hot brand on the small of her back as he urged her toward the luxury condo building. When they arrived, the doorman smiled at Nate and greeted him. She was sure Nate answered, because she felt the rumble of his deep voice like a caress against her body, but she didn't really hear the words. They walked across the marble floors in the lobby, and the sound of her Louboutin heels seemed overly loud to her when matched with the heavy footfall of Nate's boots.

"This is a really nice building," she said, inwardly smacking herself for the inane comment.

"It's part of the downtown revitalization project. Most of the city development has taken place on the outskirts, and we didn't want to lose the charm of Cole's Hill."

"It's hard to think of Cole's Hill as so…trendy and metropolitan. When I was growing up here, it felt like a tiny redneck town."

He laughed. "I bet it wasn't just the town that felt that way. Some of the people here are still good old boys, but we've got some style now."

"I can see that," she said.

They had crossed the lobby, and she noticed there were two banks of elevators. Nate steered her toward the ones on the right.

He reached around her with his free hand to hit the elevator button, and as they stepped inside the fingers of his hand dipped lower, brushing against the top of her buttocks.

She shuddered and leaned back as the elevator door closed, enveloping them in a world all their own. He used his hand to push her toward the back of the car and then he stepped in behind her, his chest pressed along her back and his free hand pressed against the wall of the car as he leaned in close to her.

"I want you, Kin," he whispered right into her ear. "It's as if I've never had you and I'm on fire for you."

She shivered again and turned her head to face him. His blue eyes were sincere and she saw there was a flush of arousal on his face.

"I want you, too," she admitted.

"Good," he said, bringing his mouth down on her lips. She opened to him, his tongue brushing over her teeth and tangling with hers. She half turned in his arms and put one hand on his face as he deepened the kiss. There was the slightest hint of a five o'clock shadow on his jaw, and she ran her fingers back and forth over the stubble as he thrust his tongue in and out of her mouth.

She tried to turn more fully into his body, but he lifted his head and stepped back just as the elevator pinged to signal their arrival on his floor. She noted that he had the timing of the ride down and hoped she wasn't making as big a mistake as she had in Vegas.

But honestly, she wanted him. It felt good to be with him, and it had been way too long since anyone had made her feel this way.

Again he put his hand right at the small of her back as they walked off the elevator and down the corridor to his apartment. She heard the lock disengage as they approached and he reached around her to open the door. She stepped inside and away from him, hoping that the break from his touch would bring some clarity.

Was she really doing this?

"Second thoughts?" he asked.

"A few, but I'm still standing right here," she said. She hadn't come up to his apartment just to turn and walk away. "But there is something I should tell you before we go any farther."

He reached for his belt buckle and slowly undid it, then drew the belt through the loops of his jeans, holding it loosely in one hand.

"I remember what you like," he said.

She blushed even harder, and a pulse of liquid desire went through her. Her fantasies had always leaned a little bit toward the dirty side, and Nate had been more than happy to play his part in them with her.

"Not that," she said.

But her mind wasn't on the secret she'd meant to share as he came closer to her. "Put your hands behind your back, Kinley," he said.

His voice was straight out of her hottest dreams, and she turned and did what he asked. He let the thick leather of his belt brush against her skin before he drew her wrists together behind her back and looped the belt around them. He tightened it, but not so firmly that she was uncomfortable. The position drew her shoulders back and pushed her breasts forward. She felt her nipples tighten against the fabric of her bra.

He wrapped one hand around the side of her neck and shoulder and pushed her slightly forward so that she was almost off balance. His other hand was at the small of her back again, gathering the fabric of the skirt of her dress and drawing it slowly up until she felt the cool air brush against the backs of her thighs and then her butt cheeks. She wore a thong, so when he lowered his hand to cup her it was bare skin on skin.

She felt another one of those liquid pulses in her

center and shivered as he held her with one hand on her neck and the other on her ass. He stroked his finger between her legs, tracing the fabric of her thong as he came back up. She felt his finger nestle in her and then skim up to where the lacy waistband was. He hooked his finger in the top of it and drew it slowly down her legs. She felt the heat of his breath against her back through the fabric of her dress, and then he moved lower, nipping against her exposed backside and then kissing the back of her knee. She tottered in her heels.

But he steadied her with both hands at her waist as he pushed her panties to the floor.

"Step out of them," he said.

She did as he commanded, and then his mouth moved back up her body, stopping to kiss and nibble wherever he wanted. He slowly stood up behind her. "Ready to watch the light show?"

She nodded, but honestly the answer was no. She was ready for him to stop teasing her and get down to business, but he just let the fabric of her skirt drop to cover her nakedness and then put his hand on the small of her back and urged her to walk toward the French doors that led to his balcony. He opened the door, and the warmth of the night surrounded her as she stepped out onto the balcony. Her arms behind her back didn't feel awkward at all as he urged her forward toward the railing. He stood behind her, and her fingers brushed over the crotch of his jeans against his erection.

She stroked him through the denim and then fumbled around until she could undo the button and zipper of his jeans. She felt his fingers brush over hers as he reached between them and freed himself from his underwear. The next thing she felt was his hands in her hair sweeping it to one side as he lowered his mouth against the back of her neck. He had one hand on the railing of the balcony and the other lifted up the back of her skirt.

She felt decadent as she realized how exposed they were on the balcony, but no one could see anything other than the two of them pressed together given the height of the balcony and the darkness. They were the only two who knew that his hands were on her naked buttocks and her hands were wrapped around his erection.

She stroked him as the music started to blare in the town square. Then his hand moved around under her skirt to her stomach. He drew her back against him, and his hard length slipped from her fingers to nestle between her legs. His fingers moved lower until he was stroking her most intimate flesh.

She rocked against him, trapped between his erection and his fingers and his mouth on her neck. He suckled the skin at the base of her neck and she shivered and shuddered in his arms. Her eyes closed as the lights in the town square dimmed and the music swelled.

He parted her and tapped his finger against her before he rubbed in a circular motion that made her legs weak. She sagged against him, and he chuckled against her skin.

"You like that?"

She nodded. Words were beyond her at this point. He pulled her back into the curve of his body, his fingers moving lower to plunge in and out of her center. She felt his erection moving between her legs and realized he was going to keep teasing her. She reached lower between his legs and cupped him, teasing him with her fingers and then scraping her nails over the lower part of his shaft until he drew his hips back and took his fingers from between her legs.

She felt his hands on the belt that held her wrists together and then it was off. Before she could do anything, he took both of her hands in his and put them on the railing in front of them. She wrapped her hands around the cool wrought iron and canted her hips back toward him.

Below the images flashed on city hall and the music swelled, but there was a storm brewing inside her that put all of that to shame. Nate had one hand on the small of her back under the fabric of her dress and she turned around to look at him, seeing him holding a condom packet in one hand.

He ripped it open and put it on with one hand then pulled her hips back toward his. She felt his erection slide against her most intimate flesh and then he entered her. He stretched her as he thrust into her, and his other hand went between her legs to fondle her clit. She moaned and tried to make him move inside her, but his hips stayed still as his one finger tapped out a rhythm against her. His mouth was against the side of her neck, and she groaned as she felt her orgasm approaching. She wanted to stop it from coming, but it had been too long and he felt too good.

She groaned again as her climax washed over her and everything inside her clenched, squeezing his erection. He continued to rub her. He started to move, slowly pulling out of her and then plunging back in, deeply. He moved slowly at first and then started going more quickly. She turned her head, trying to find his mouth, and he accommodated her, kissing the side of her neck and then her jaw as he continued to drive himself deep inside her until she felt that tingling along her body and she knew she was about to come again. She did as he continued thrusting and then he gripped her hips, driving hard into her with more intensity. Then she felt him shudder against her back and moan against her neck. He thrust into her a few more times and then wrapped one arm tight around her stomach, holding her to him as he put his other hand on the railing next to hers.

The kisses he dropped on her neck now were softer as he cradled her to him. She closed her eyes and stood there, wrapped in his arms. He was still inside her as the light show concluded.

He finally pulled himself free of her body and then lifted her in his arms, carrying her back into the apartment. She wrapped her arms around his shoulders, put her head against his chest and closed her eyes.

There was no running away from this night and her actions, and she was honest with herself, admitting she wasn't ready to leave him. Not yet. But she knew she had to talk to him.

She had to tell him about Penny. But when he put her on her feet in the living room, she found it was harder than ever to find the words. She wobbled a little for a second. She felt the moisture between her legs and knew she should excuse herself to go clean up. She caught a glimpse of herself in the mirror and was surprised to see how normal she looked. Her clothes were still in place, her hair just a tiny bit rumpled, but otherwise she looked the same as she had at dinner.

She was the only one who knew how much she'd

changed. That the storm that was Nate had once again swept through her life and this time was more unsettling than the last. She hadn't known what she was letting herself in for the last time, but this time…there was no excuse.

He had tucked himself back into his pants and zipped them but left the button undone. His shirt was untucked… He looked more unkempt than she did.

She wanted to believe that this was more than just something physical, but she wasn't naive. Not where he was concerned. He had been too practiced…well, in the elevator. On the balcony that hadn't felt like a routine.

"I missed the light show," she said at last. She glanced around for her purse and saw she'd dropped it by the door, but she didn't remember that. She'd been so focused on Nate when they'd entered his apartment she was only just now taking notice of the decor. It was modern and masculine. There was a Georgia O'Keeffe painting of skulls that dominated the living room wall mounted above a riverstone fireplace. The ceilings were high and vaulted.

"Should I apologize?" he asked. "I hope you still enjoyed yourself."

"You know I did," she said.

He brushed past her, walking toward the kitchen, which was nestled against the wall and opened into the living room. He went to the fridge and took out a bottle of sparkling water before coming back to the breakfast bar and getting two glasses and filling them with water.

"Do you wish things had been different?" he asked.

She shrugged. "I don't regret this."

"Good," he said, holding out one of the glasses to her. She walked over, took it from him and had a sip. "I meant to wait until later, but there is something about you, Kinley…like I said at dinner, you're different from everyone else."

She felt that same spark of hope that this was more than just a good time, but she ruthlessly shoved it back down. One night wasn't going to change Nate any more than one night could change her… But one night had. One night in Vegas had altered her life and made her into the woman she was today.

So one night could have a huge impact.

Was that what was going on with Nate?

She needed to tell him about Penny. Now, so that if this really was a different Nate they'd have a chance to be together. Forever. Or he could let her know that he wasn't interested.

"Do you want to spend the night?" he asked.

"Do you want me to?" she countered. But she knew she couldn't. In fact, this was the perfect opening for her to finally come clean about her daughter. "Don't answer that. I can't stay the night. I have to get home."

"Why?" he asked. "No one is going to be upset if you stay here with me."

She took a deep breath and put her glass down on the countertop. "I have a daughter."

There, she'd said it.

"A daughter?"

"Yes. Her name is Penny, and she's two years old."

He rubbed the back of his neck. "Well, that is a complication."

"It doesn't have to be," she said. "I just thought you should know."

She felt better having told him. He must know by the age that Penny was his.

"I'm guessing the dad is out of the picture."

She stared at him for a moment. Did he think she'd slept with someone else so quickly after she'd been with him?

"Yeah, he is," she said at last. Realizing that even though she thought she knew Nate, he had no clue about her at all. Though she'd partied hard with him, she'd never given herself cheaply or easily to anyone...but Nate.

She was too stunned to say anything else to him or try to explain. How could he think so little of her? Or miss the obvious: that Penny was his daughter.

Six

Memorial Day was a big celebration in Cole's Hill. All of the businesses on Main Street had flags flying and patriotic displays in their front windows. Kinley and Penny were joined by Pippa as they searched for a good spot to see the annual Memorial Day parade.

"I've never been to a parade before," Penny said in a very singsongy voice. From the moment that Penny had woken up this morning she'd been singing everything. She'd insisted on wearing her newest T-shirt that had a horse on it with her red, white and blue–striped shorts. It didn't match and Kinley had thought about arguing with her daughter about her clothing choices but then asked herself why it mattered what Penny wore if the outfit made her happy. So she let her wear it.

"Me, either," Pippa said. Her nanny, a twenty-three-year-old from the UK, had dyed her hair red and blue on the tips in support of Memorial Day.

"Well, I have, and y'all are in for a treat," Kinley said. She led the way toward the studio Jacs had rented for them to use for their business, which was along the parade route. They set up the portable chairs they'd been carrying for the adults and placed a thick picnic blanket on the ground between the chairs for Penny. Kinley started to get settled in when she noticed Bianca and her son walking toward them.

"Hey! Do you mind if we sit with you?" Bianca asked as she approached.

"Not at all," Kinley said. "Bianca, this is Pippa, who helps out with Penny. And this is my daughter, Penny. Everyone, this is Bianca."

"Hiya," Pippa said with a wave.

"Hello," Penny said. "Who's that?"

She pointed to Bianca's son, getting up from her chair and moving closer.

"This is Benito," Bianca said.

Penny and Benito stared at each other for a few minutes and then Kinley heard her daughter start talking about horses. She offered to let Benito share her blanket and her toys.

"May I, mama?" Benito asked.

"Si, changuita," Bianca said, kissing her son on the head as the two kids settled on the blanket.

Bianca set her chair up next to Kinley's.

"Did you just call your son little monkey?" Kinley asked trying to remember the Spanish she'd heard growing up.

"Yes. My *papi* used to call us that when we were little," Bianca said.

"I think I'm going to take a walk while we're waiting for the parade to start and see what the town has to offer," Pippa said. "Wanna come with me, imp?"

"No, Pippy, I'm playing with my new friend," Penny said.

"He can come, too," Pippa said.

"Wanna go?" Penny asked Benito.

He leaned around Penny and looked over at Bianca, who nodded at him. *"Si."*

"Si? What's that mean?" Penny asked.

"Yes," he said. They both clambered to their feet and Pippa held out her hands to the kids, leading them toward some of the tents that had been set up along the parade route.

"What happened the other night with Nate Caruthers?" Bianca asked as soon as they were alone. "Are you two dating?"

Kinley should have been ready to have people ask about her and Nate. Cole's Hill was getting big and more cosmopolitan, but the Five Families all knew each other's business and Nate and Bianca were both part of that group.

"I don't know," she answered honestly, though she probably should have said no and then meant it. She couldn't date a man who was the father of her child but didn't know it.

Of course, that was easier to commit to when Nate wasn't around and she wasn't thinking about him. Just thinking about the other night made her pulse race and her skin feel more sensitive. She remembered everything they'd done together. For a moment she wished she'd never brought Penny up and had spent the night with him.

"That sounds interesting," Bianca said. "If I'm being too nosy just tell me, but I'm so tired of only talking about shows on PBS Kids and I need something adult and gossipy to remind me there is life outside of my son."

Kinley laughed. "You should start working. I think it's the only thing that saved me when Penny was born. I mean, I had to work—not like you—but it gave me something to think about instead of worrying if I could raise her on my own."

"My parents have suggested I start working as well, which is why I'm interviewing at the Caruthers, Parker and Zevon Surgical Group on Monday. I remember how much your job changed you," Bianca said. "The tone in your emails changed. You seemed…in a better place."

"I was," Kinley said. It was ironic that the job that had saved her from dwelling on Nate and his absence in her life was directly responsible for bringing them back together. "Benito is cute as a button."

"So is Penny. She seems to really love horses," Bianca said. "Have you had her out at the Rockin' C?"

"No. Not yet. I've been busy with the wedding planning. Jacs didn't want to send me out here for just one client and has been arranging for new clients all over the state. I'm pretty sure she has no idea how big the state of Texas is. She wanted me to drive down to Galveston to check out a venue in the morning and see a client in Dallas for lunch."

Bianca laughed. "Did you set her straight?"

"I tried," Kinley said. "But she mentioned she was trying to find me a private plane so I could get to all the appointments. Next week is going to be very busy for me."

"Wow, sounds like it. Don't you miss Penny when you're traveling for work?" Bianca asked.

Kinley knew her friend meant well and wasn't being critical of her, but she still felt a twinge of guilt…something she thought all working mothers must experience. "I do miss her, which is why Jacs is arranging for the plane. She knows that I like to be home every night for either dinner or bedtime with Penny."

"I didn't mean anything by that," Bianca said. "Everyone keeps telling me to give Beni some breathing space and to get a job. Mainly because of everything with Jose's death. They think it's not healthy for either of us. No one really gets what it's like to be the only one there for him."

"I do. From the moment I found out I was pregnant it's just been me. Sometimes I don't make the best decisions, but they are the only ones I can make," she said. The guilt that had been a knot in her stomach since she'd returned loosened a little bit.

"That's really all we can do. I didn't realize Penny's father had been gone from the beginning. Is he dead?" Bianca asked.

"No. He just didn't want to listen when I tried to tell him he had a child," Kinley said.

Luckily Pippa and the kids came back then so she could stop thinking about Nate and how she was going to tell him about Penny. And what impact that was going to have on all of their lives.

Memorial Day was a huge deal on the Rockin' C ranch. Everyone had been given the day off after the morning chores were completed. After all, cattle didn't know it was a holiday. Most of the ranch hands and their families were in town watching the Cole's Hill annual parade and then they would be back for a barbecue by the Samson Lake. One of Nate's ancestors had named the lake after he'd been wronged by a woman and felt like Samson.

The lake had started life as a fishing hole and been dug out and expanded to its current size, which was big enough for fishing and water sports. A creek that ran off a spur of the Guadalupe River fed it. There was a dock with seating for about twenty and two speedboats that were set up for taking the ranch staff and the families out tubing or water skiing.

Marcus Quinten, Kinley's dad, was in charge of the annual fest and was supervising his team at the grills. Nate had stayed behind to help out as well but also because he'd wanted to talk to Marcus and try to learn more about the guy who had fathered Kinley's child.

Marcus was getting older and his brown hair was mostly gray now. He was still one of the strongest men on the ranch, but at fifty-two he was getting a little soft around the middle. He shaved every Sunday, so today he was clean shaven but by the end of the week stubble would be covering his cheeks. He was a genius with horses, and there were days when Nate thought that Marcus could forget more about ranching in a day than he'd ever know in a lifetime.

"Just get the pits going," Marcus said as Nate walked over to him. Marcus had served in the military right after high school, just one stint before coming to Cole's Hill and being hired on a ranch hand. "I think this year is going to be one of our best. Our beef was superb this year."

"We got top dollar for it. Your new breeding and grazing program is paying off. Thanks," Nate said.

"That's what you pay me for, son," Marcus said.

A twinge of guilt went through him at Marcus's nickname for him. He hadn't been a very good honorary son to Marcus. Not when it came to Kinley. He had a lot of respect and admiration for Marcus, but there had always been that crazy, wild part of him that he'd never been able to control.

"Marcus, mind if I ask you a question?"

"Not at all," Marcus said, straightening his cowboy hat. He looked over at Nate with those same dark brown eyes that Kinley had.

"What do you know about the father of Kinley's kid?" Nate asked.

Marcus inhaled sharply and then put his hands on his hips. "Why do you want to know?"

"I like your daughter. I'd like to ask her out, but I wanted to make sure there wasn't someone else in the picture," Nate said, which was pretty damned close to the truth.

Marcus nodded slowly and then gestured for Nate

to follow him, leading him away from the ranch hands who were tending the grills. Marcus walked up the dock and stood there at the end staring out at the lake. The sound of the water lapping against the pilings that held the dock up was the only thing to break the silence.

Finally Marcus turned to him. "I don't know a damned thing about the father. Only that when she asked him if he wanted to be a part of their lives, he said no. She's been on her own since."

Nate thought that guy must be a big asshole to not want to be in his kid's life but then wondered how he would have reacted almost three years ago if she'd told him he was going to be the father of a child. He hadn't been ready to settle down or even be serious about one woman.

"What a jerk," Nate said.

"Well, I had some other words I used to describe him, but that works," Marcus said, turning to fully face Nate. "I don't mind if you date my daughter, Nathaniel. I've known you since you were born and you might be a little wild, but underneath all that I've always believed you are a decent man. But she's been screwed over enough, so make sure whatever your intentions are, she knows them up front. I won't hesitate to come after you like I wanted to go after the sumbitch that knocked her up and left her behind."

Nate respected that. He had no intention of leading Kinley on. He didn't know what the future held for the two of them but he intended to let her know exactly what he wanted right from the start.

"Fair enough, sir."

Penny ended up sitting on Kinley's lap during most of the parade, while Bianca held Benito. Kinley watched the parade and felt a keen sense of longing for her hometown, which was silly, since she was sitting right here in it. But she knew that in six months she'd be heading back to Las Vegas and her old life.

While Vegas was very good at putting on a show, there was nothing like this. She had seen people she'd known as a kid and new friends she'd made through Penny's day care. She had a sense of civic pride that she hadn't realized she was missing. This town felt like a community, one she wanted to be a part of.

It would be difficult to start a business on her own and just move here. So she wasn't sure what she really wanted. Plus there was the fact that she might not really want to stay, depending on Nate's reaction when she told him about Penny. But for this moment she wished she could.

As the parade ended, Kinley gathered together their stuff while Benito and Penny both continued talking to each other and comparing the candy and toys they'd caught during the parade.

"Mama, can I go with Benito to a barbie?" Penny asked.

"Do you mean a barbecue?" Kinley asked her daughter, smiling down at her.

She nodded vigorously, her red ponytail bobbing up and down.

Kinley glanced over at Bianca. "Are you having people over?"

"Not me. We are going to the Rockin' C barbecue. Aren't you going?" Bianca asked.

Her father was in charge of the annual event and had asked them to come out there for it. But since she'd been trying to figure out how to tell Nate about his daughter before he met Penny, she'd thought she should skip it.

"I wasn't going to."

Bianca shrugged. "It's up to you, but my brothers are going to be there. If you aren't going to date Nate, maybe one of them will interest you."

Kinley shook her head. Life was crazy enough already without adding another guy to the mix. "I remember your brothers when they used to torment us as kids."

"They've turned out pretty good," Bianca said with a wink. "I know how to keep them in line now."

"I bet you do," Kinley said.

"Mama? Can we go?" Penny asked, tugging on the hem of Kinley's shorts.

She looked down into her daughter's face and saw the hope and expectation and wanted to say yes. But she was afraid.

It was the first time in a really long time that she'd felt this kind of fear. The last time had been right after she'd brought Penny home from the hospital and her daughter wouldn't stop crying all night. Kinley had been scared that she would ruin Penny's life with her ignorance when it came to mothering.

"Hmm… I'm not sure. We had plans to go to the movies this afternoon," Kinley said. "Are you sure you want to miss that?"

"Yes," Penny said. "I really, really, really want to go."

Knowing that Bianca would probably be suspicious if she made up some excuse not to go out to the Rockin' C and might even ask questions that Kinley didn't want to answer, she decided to give in. She'd try to locate Nate and talk to him before he saw Penny.

"Okay."

"Yay! Thank you, Mama," Penny said, throwing her arms around Kinley's legs and hugging her tightly. Penny turned back to Benito. "I can go."

The two kids chatted all the way up Main Street

and it was only when they got to the cars that they hugged each other and waved goodbye.

Pippa helped Kinley buckle Penny into the car seat and then turned to her out of earshot of her daughter. "I thought we were avoiding the Rockin' C at all costs."

"We were. But I didn't want to make Bianca think I was avoiding something. It's bad enough that Dad is on me for not coming out to the ranch," Kinley said. "I'm going to try to find Nate and tell him when we get there. Do you mind keeping a close eye on Penny? I imagine she's going to want to hang out with Benito."

"I got your back, Kin. Whatever you need, I'll be there for you and Penny. You two are like family to me."

Impulsively Kinley hugged Pippa. "It's the same for us. I don't know how I would have managed the last two years without you."

"To be honest, me, either," Pippa said. "Now let's go see what a real American barbecue is like. I've never been to one."

"It's loud and fun and hot. The food will be delicious and I recommend you try it all. My dad has a secret rub he makes for the meat…he's really good at that," Kinley said.

They got in the car and started to drive out to the ranch. Penny was playing an interactive game on her tablet and wearing her headphones as they drove.

"You don't talk about him much," Pippa said.

"I know," Kinley said. She and her dad had been close until her mom had moved them to California after the divorce. After her mom died, they'd started talking again, and maybe they would have had a chance to be closer if it weren't for that weekend with Nate.

After Nate had told her what happened in Vegas needed to stay there, Kinley had been too embarrassed to think of visiting Cole's Hill and her father ever again. And of course having Penny had just given her one more reason to stay away. Her father had come to Vegas twice but those were always very brief visits usually around the Professional Bull Riding finals that were always in Vegas.

"He's a good guy and wants to protect me and Penny. But I know I can't tell him about Nate, because it could cost him his job. Which is the last thing I'd want. So I've kept him at arm's length."

"That secret is taking over your entire life," Pippa said. "Just like mine did before I ran away from England. Are you sick of it? I know I am."

"Yes. But telling the truth is harder than I ever thought it would be."

Seven

The DJ had been flown in from Nashville and was blasting a mix of old country classics that had formed the soundtrack to Nate's childhood, like George Jones, Bocephus and Willie Nelson, as well as newer artists like Florida Georgia Line, Zac Brown Band and Kenny Chesney. Right now "Sinner" was playing, and he and his brothers were all doing their rowdiest singing along with Aaron Lewis while their dad chimed in on Willie Nelson's parts.

Nate had spent the morning on the water, taking kids and ranch hands tubing behind the speedboat. He'd lost his shirt along the way and as the afternoon lengthened into twilight he had started drinking. He'd caught a glimpse of Kinley earlier, but his talk with Marcus had made him realize that rushing things with her probably wasn't a good idea.

His dad had his long hair pulled back in a pony-tail and looked like the redneck hippie he'd always been. He had been drinking hard as well, and when the song changed to George Jones's "He Stopped Loving Her Today," his mom had come to grab his dad and claim a dance. Nate and his brothers just sat down on the edge of one of the bales of hay that had been set up around the dance floor and watched them.

"Look at them. Still crazy for each other after all these years," Ethan said. There was a hint of wist-fulness in his voice.

Nate felt that same longing deep inside, and he realized that all his running around had been to fill up the need for this thing his parents had found. He hadn't really recognized that until this moment. He scanned the crowds and saw Kinley again on the other side of the dance floor talking to Hector Velas-quez. Then she threw her head back and laughed at something Hector said and Nate was on his feet before he realized what he was doing.

He didn't stop as he wove his way through the crowd and over to where Kinley was.

"Excuse me, Hector, the lady and I are going to

dance," Nate said, putting his hand on Kinley's hip and turning her toward the dance floor.

"We are?" she asked as he pulled her into his arms and started doing his version of a country waltz around the dance floor.

God, he'd missed her. Her face showed the effects of being out in the sun all day, and a few tendrils of her red hair had escaped her braids and curled around her face and neck.

She wore a pair of white shorts that ended midthigh and showed off her legs. They were long and skinny and he remembered exactly how good it had felt when he was between them. His erection stirred as he danced her around to the music, and he realized that this was what he'd been missing in his life—this feeling of excitement that he only got when he was with Kinley.

"Yes, ma'am," he said. "I owe you something nice after the way things ended the other night."

"I don't think you owe me anything," she said. "Actually, I was hoping to run into you today."

"You were?" he asked, pulling her closer to him as the music changed to "Sangria" by Blake Shelton. Nate put his hands on her hips as she wrapped her arms around his shoulders. Nate lowered his head toward hers and looked down into her eyes. He wanted her. He might have had a few too many beers this afternoon, but nothing was clouding his judgment right now.

"I was. I wanted to talk to you again."

"I want something from you, too," he said, kissing her neck as he danced them off the floor toward a secluded area away from the crowd where they could still hear the music.

She looked up at him. "I'd like that, too."

"Good. We always seem to be on the same page romantically," he said. It was one of the things he really liked about Kinley. She wasn't coy about wanting him and never played games.

"We do. But we need to talk first," she said. "I don't want it to be like last time."

He didn't, either.

"Where's your daughter?" he asked.

"She went with Bianca. Her son is about Penny's age and they wanted to hang out."

"I'm looking forward to meeting her. But let's find somewhere to talk." He took Kinley's hand and led her farther from the crowds down the path that wrapped around the lake. He was careful to stay on the lighted path as he led the way to the old homestead cabin.

"Where are we going?"

"Somewhere we can be alone," he said. "Do you remember the old homestead cabin?"

"That creaky, falling-apart shack that you and your brothers used to dare me to go into?" she asked.

"Yeah, that one. A few years ago we had it re-done. It's still rustic and authentic-looking, but it no longer creaks and has all the modern conveniences. I lived in it for a while," Nate said.

"Why?"

"Dad and I were butting heads about the business and fighting a lot. It was before I bought the penthouse in town," Nate said.

"What were you fighting about?"

"Dad was stuck in the old ways of doing business. He sent me to business school and I have an MBA, but he was still treating me like his second in command even though I…well, I wanted to be in charge. Finally, he decided to retire and then I took over."

"When was that?" she asked.

"Right about when I got back from that weekend in Vegas with you, Kin," Nate said. "He decided to step down, and I knew it was going to take a lot of work to make the changes I wanted at the ranch and in the Rockin' C business. Not making excuses for what I said to you, but I just wanted you to know where I was in my life back then."

Kinley's heart was beating too fast as she stepped into the cabin after Nate. She wanted to tell him where she'd been in her life, but the words just wouldn't come. He went to turn on the air-conditioning as she looked around the one-room cabin. It had been enlarged and the kitchen was to the right of the door, with an old 1950s stove against the wall and an open-front china hutch. There were mugs and matching blue-and-white plates in the slots above them. There was a chandelier with wicker lamp shades that complimented the wrought-iron base over the butcher-block island in the kitchen.

She turned to her left and saw a king-size bed with a wrought-iron headboard and a thick hunter's plaid bedspread on it. She skipped past the bed, but her pulse had sped up at the sight of it.

Next was a fireplace that would be cozy in winter with two rocking chairs positioned in front of it, and then an antique postmaster's desk in the corner with a big leather chair.

"I like it. It's not creepy at all," she said. "Looks like it's your little love nest."

Nate rubbed the back of his neck. "I'm not going to lie to you, Kinley. I've had a lot of women in here over the years, but since you…well, it hasn't been the same. Every time I close my eyes, I've seen you."

She wanted to believe that. She wanted it more than she wanted just about anything else, but she'd been lied to before. She'd bought his lines one time…though to be fair, he'd never promised her anything other than a weekend. It had been her own hopeful heart that had painted in the rest of that fantasy, weaving her hopes and dreams into something Nate wasn't able to provide.

But he was here now.

She wanted to tell him the truth about Penny but the words were trapped in her throat.

He stood there in a pair of navy swim trunks that hung off his hips. His chest was bare, suntanned and muscled from a lifetime of work. He looked more like a cowboy today than the CEO she'd seen in town, but either way he was Nate Caruthers, the one man who was more like her Achilles' heel than she wanted to admit.

"It doesn't matter. I was just being difficult because when I'm around you all the stuff I tell myself I'm not going to do, I end up doing," she said.

She knew she couldn't be with him again. Not until she told him about Penny. But he had tipped his head to the side and canted his hips toward her as he stood there watching her.

"Did you promise yourself you wouldn't let me kiss you?"

He was hard to resist. She arched both eyebrows at him and tried to look prim and proper. "Yes, I did."

"I guess I should be a gentleman and not try to

tempt you," he said, walking toward her with intent in his eyes.

"You should," she said, but she took a step forward to meet him. And then they were standing close together, as close as when they'd been dancing, and she could smell his cologne and his sweat and the faintest whiff of barbecue sauce. He lowered his head toward hers and she had plenty of time to back away, but she wanted this. She wanted to be with Nate one more time before she told him about Penny and everything changed.

She knew some people might say she was being selfish, but she'd taken very little for herself in the last three years. She had focused on raising Penny and starting a career, and she wanted this for herself. The other night on the balcony had been fire and passion.

This was deliberate. It was her taking what she wanted with Nate because she had missed him. His mouth was full and sensual and he moved it over hers with intent, his hands skimming up and down her back as he drew her closer to him.

Their hips brushed against each other, and she felt the tip of his erection rub over her center. He was humming the song they'd danced to as he moved his body against hers, and she realized that she was starting to fall for him.

He was complex and complicated and absolutely

the last thing she needed in her life at this moment, but she wanted him—and even more important, she liked him. She could see a future for herself and Nate together once she finally told him about their daughter.

What if he rejected her when he found out that he was Penny's father? What if he couldn't understand why she'd kept silent? What if he didn't realize that telling him now was the only option she had left? She pulled her mouth from his and looked up into those blue-gray eyes, and her heartbeat was so loud in her ears that she couldn't hear Nate when he spoke.

"What?"

"Isn't that what you wanted from me?" he asked.

It was. But she knew the guilt inside her would keep on growing unless she told him her secret.

"It is. But I wanted to talk to you. I have something you need to hear first," she said. "It's important."

He took her hand in his and drew it to his chest. He held it over his heart, and she felt the steady beat under her hand. He rubbed her hand over his body, down over his rib cage and his rock-hard stomach and lower, to his erection.

"More important than this?" he asked then pulled her back into his arms, kissing her slowly and deeply and seducing her with his body.

His kisses said not to worry about anything and that this was going to make everything okay between them. And though she knew it wouldn't, she wrapped her hand around his erection and her free arm around his shoulders and met his passion with her own.

Talking had never made anything better as far as Nate was concerned. Especially not with Kinley. He lifted her off her feet, one arm right under her buttocks and the other around her back, swung her around and walked toward the bed. He'd been living here when they'd hooked up in Vegas, and in the nightstand was a picture of the two of them from their first night together. They'd gone into one of those photo booths and he had a strip of four photos of the two of them. He tried to avoid looking at it, because it had always stirred up regret. Despite what he'd told her, he hadn't brought any other women here. This place reminded him of the time he'd had with Kinley in Vegas, and the last thing he'd wanted to do was to have another woman interfere with that.

He turned so that he sat down on the edge of the bed and she straddled his lap. Lifting his mouth from hers, he reached for the buttons of her blouse and undid them slowly.

She put her hands on his shoulders at first as he

took her blouse off and undid her bra before tossing it aside. Her skin was so soft and creamy and her torso was covered in freckles. He leaned forward, licking one of the bigger ones just above her left breast. He put his hands on her tiny waist and rubbed his thumbs up and down against her body.

She sat back on his thighs, her shoulders back and her spine arched, and he looked at her and caught his breath. Logically he knew there might be women as beautiful as her in the world, but when he looked at her, for the life of him, he couldn't remember seeing anyone as breathtaking as Kinley.

His hands looked too big and rough as he caressed the side of her neck and then her collarbone. He drew his finger down her arm and noticed that her nipple beaded as his hand came closer to her breast. She shifted on his lap as he cupped one breast in his hand and leaned forward to lightly lick her nipple.

She put her hands on either side of his head and held him to her. Her back arched even more, and her hips were rubbing against his thighs. She made a soft little sound in the back of her throat that drove him wild.

His swim trunks were too tight against his erection, and he lifted his head and shifted her off his lap to her feet. He undid the button latch of her shorts and then slowly lowered the zipper, drawing her shorts and then her panties down her legs. She stepped out of both of them. Her hands went to the tie fastening of his swim trunks, and soon they were both naked. He lifted her back onto his lap as he sat back down on the bed.

She scooted forward and wrapped her arm around his shoulders as the tip of his erection nestled against her center. She was warm and wet and ready for him and it was only as he felt her nakedness on him that he realized he didn't have a condom close by.

"Dammit," he said. "Wrap your arms and legs around me."

She did as he asked, and he stood up and walked the short distance to the bathroom, which was the only room with a door in the open-plan cabin. He set her down on the countertop as he reached around her to the medicine cabinet and found the box of condoms there. He shook one out and Kinley caught it.

She tore open the packet and put the condom on him and then shifted so that he was poised at the opening of her body. He made a shallow thrust into her and then drew back, lowering his mouth to her nipple and sucking on it as he drove his hips forward, plunging fully into her body this time.

He felt her nails on his back and her legs tighten around his hips as the rhythm between them intensified. He put one hand between their bodies and rubbed her clit as he kept up the pace until he felt her tightening around him. Shivers went down his spine and he lifted his head from her breasts, tightening his hold on her as their mouths found each other.

He sucked her tongue into his mouth as he drove into her harder and faster. She bit the tip of his tongue and tore her mouth from his, crying out his name. He felt her clamping down on him.

Every muscle in his body was tense and he was driving into her, focused on the sensation of her long limbs wrapped around him and her center pulsing around his length. Then he felt that feathering along his spine as he started to come. He buried his face against her neck and pushed into her three more times until he felt empty.

He kept thrusting a few more times because it felt so good. Her arms loosened around his shoulders and she stroked her hands up and down his back. When he turned his head on her shoulder, she was looking down at hm.

There was something in her eyes that looked like…well, he wasn't too sure, but it was a mix of sensual satisfaction and something a little bit like apprehension. He wondered if she was worried he'd ask more questions about her past.

He hated to see that look on her face, so he lifted her off the sink and carried her to his bed and held her in his arms. He just held her, not talking, until he started to drift off to sleep. He wasn't sure how long he slept, but when he woke Kinley was gone and he was alone again.

Eight

Kinley was so ready to be back in Las Vegas. Especially after the other night with Nate, when she'd left him sleeping at the cabin because she'd chickened out. Since then she'd been busy with work, and if she were being completely honest, with avoiding him. She'd stayed away from the downtown area where she knew his offices were. So when the opportunity to fly with a few of her brides-to-be to Vegas for dress shopping arose, she'd jumped on it.

Penny and her nanny made the trip as well. Now they were back in Kinley's home in Henderson enjoying playdates with Penny's friends and giving Pippa a chance to meet up with some of her friends.

Ferrin, Joie, who was engaged to the professional basketball player, and Meredith, who's fiancé was a Dallas Cowboy, along with their closest friends, mothers and soon-to-be mothers-in-law were all staying in suites at the Chimera Hotel, and Kinley had about thirty minutes before the brides were due to arrive. They'd landed last night and Kinley had been in Jacs's showroom since six this morning getting it set up for the dress shopping. They had accounts with all of the major designers, and since Jacs did a lot of business with them, they were always sent the latest designs.

Kinley thought it was funny that she worked as a wedding planner since the bride fantasy had never really been one of hers. She'd been a tomboy more into daydreaming about winning a rodeo buckle or living on an island with wild horses than planning her perfect wedding day.

But as she moved through a sea of ivory, cream and pure white dresses, fingering the satin and lace, she did sort of feel a little bit of longing. Since the moment she'd hung up the phone with Nate a few years ago and realized that he wasn't going to be in her life, she'd focused on having her baby and being a single mom.

She thought she'd put away her dreams of a white wedding with all of her friends and family looking on, but she was starting to wish it was her trying on dresses.

"Well, kid, looks like Texas didn't kill you," Jacs said as she swept into the room in a cloud of Chanel perfume wearing an all-white pantsuit and waving her manicured fingers at Kinley.

Kinley turned to look at her boss, trying to school her features into something confident and nonchalant. But she noticed the concern on Jacs's face and realized she hadn't been quick enough.

"What happened?"

"Nothing that matters to the job. I'm killing it as a bridal planner," Kinley said.

Jacs put her arm around Kinley's shoulders and drew her over to one of the love seats that had been positioned all over the room. There were actually five dressing rooms in this area and each would be used for a different bridal party. The teams from the design houses would be making their way through the rooms so that each bride would have private attention.

"What happened?"

Kinley looked at Jacs. She was her boss, but they were also friends. "I don't think you'd understand. I made another one of the stupid, impulsive decisions that will have consequences, and I don't know how to fix it."

"Why wouldn't I understand?" Jacs asked.

"Because you're smart."

Jacs threw her head back and laughed with that loud, booming sound that made Kinley smile despite the fact that her life was one big mess at the moment.

"I wish I was as smart as you think I am. I'm guessing this problem involves a man, given that you didn't want to go to Texas and now you're saying things are a mess."

She took a deep breath and held it.

"You really don't want me to get into this," Kinley said.

"Hon, you are more than an employee. When you came in here looking for a job with just your sense of style and that tiny baby, I took a chance on you because I saw something more—a determination to make a good life for yourself and your baby. There's nothing you can say that will change my opinion of you," Jacs said.

"Penny's father is one of our clients' brothers. I never told him," Kinley said, looking down at her hands and neatly crossed legs. There were no chips in her manicure. If only she were as calm and put together on the inside as she was on the outside.

"Did you try to tell him? Is he an ass? Is this a problem? Will it affect our client's wedding?"

Jacs's quick-fire questions made Kinley's head spin. "Yes. Sometimes. Yes. And I hope not," she answered. "I thought telling him about Penny and how old she was would make him realize she was his daughter and if not, I'd just tell him. But instead he asked me if the dad was still in the picture… Jacs, he thought I was with another guy almost at the same time I was with him."

Jacs squeezed her closed. "Men can be dimwitted. Maybe he didn't realize when you would have had to be pregnant to have Penny. You should try to tell again."

Kinley nodded. "I know. I'm planning to. And it's even more complicated, because Nate's mom is so sweet and she told me how she wants grandchildren and I know she has one…"

Jacs put her hands on Kinley's as she nervously twisted her fingers together. It was funny that Kinley had been able to be confident when she was by herself, but having her friend and mentor here with her gave her a chance to talk about all the things that were weighing on her mind.

"She is always going to have that grandchild. You already said you are going to let the father know, and then she will have a chance to build the relationship. If there is one thing I know for sure about you, Kinley Quinten, it's that you are unstoppable when you make up your mind. You'll make this work."

She knew Jacs was right. A lot of people—her friends and even her dad—had expressed concern about her being able to raise a child on her own, but she hadn't let them dissuade her from having her daughter and finding a well-paying job. And on most days she did a really good job of being a mother.

"You're right. Thanks, Jacs. I needed that."

Jacs winked at her as she stood up. "We all need someone in our corner who sees our strengths. It's way too easy for us to focus on the negatives at times. I've got Willa coming in and I'm here to help out, too. Which one of us do you want with which bride?"

Kinley and Jacs finished talking business and were ready when the first bride arrived. It was Ferrin, accompanied by her mom and Nate's mom, along with Ferrin's maid of honor, Gabi de la Cruz. This time Kinley didn't feel swamped by guilt when she saw Ma Caruthers, and as she shepherded the party into one of the dressing rooms she noticed Jacs watching her and gave her friend the thumbs-up sign. She would figure out how to make this work. As Jacs had said, she was smart and capable. But somehow all of those things seemed to fly out the window when Nate was in the picture.

Los Angeles was a far cry from Cole's Hill, and as much as Nate loved to travel, he was glad this was his last night away from Texas. He had come to

Ethan's Beverly Hills office to sign a new contract with a long-running television series that liked to use part of the Rockin' C for exterior shots and some on-location filming. He was having dinner tonight with Ethan and Hunter at a trendy new restaurant. A few of his brothers' friends—Kingsley Buchanan and Manu Barrett, whom Hunter knew from his NFL playing days, and Hayden McBride, a partner in the same firm as Ethan—had joined them.

The group was boisterous. There was a lot of good-natured teasing of King and Hunter, who were both recently engaged. King had an adorable three-year-old son who was spending the month was his maternal grandparents. Nate had caught a glimpse of Conner, King's son, earlier when King and Hunter had video called him. Hunter was very close to them both.

Nate had never paid much attention to kids, but given that Kinley was still on his mind and now that he'd had a week to think about things, he realized he should have talked to her more about her daughter after she'd brought the subject up. He was jealous of the man who was the baby's father. It seemed to him that he must have had a powerful hold on Kinley to talk her into bed after Nate had left Vegas… and, well, rejected her.

"Tell me about being a dad," Nate said to King

once dinner was over and they'd arrived at a cigar club Manu had recommended.

"What do you want to know?"

Nate shrugged. "I'm sort of dating a girl who has a kid."

"Wow. That's not like you at all," King said.

"Which is why I'm asking you about kids," Nate said. Already he was regretting this. It wouldn't be long until King told Hunter and then Hunter would tell his brothers and everyone would know about him and Kinley. Not that he was hiding her or anything, but he would have liked to have sorted things out privately before his entire family guessed that he had a thing for her.

"What do I need to know? She said her daughter is two. The dad is out of the picture…hell, I'm not really even sure when he was last in the picture."

"Did you ask her about him?"

"Just if he was still around. Why?" Nate asked, leaning back against the thickly upholstered bench and taking a puff of his cigar.

"Women always wanted to know about Conner's mom. I think they were being careful to make sure she wasn't still in the picture. I was pretty up front about everything, telling them I was a widower, mentioning the cloud of doubt that was hanging around me from the Frat House Murder."

Hunter's college girlfriend had been murdered

after a frat party and Hunter and his best friend Kingsley had been questioned in connection to the crime. The culprit hadn't been caught for ten years and the stigma of the suspicion of being a murderer had hung around King and Hunter until the actual murderer had been caught last year.

"She said she had a kid and I asked if the dad was still in the picture. I didn't want to know too much about the dude since I'm pretty sure Kinley hooked up with him after—" Nate broke off. He hadn't meant to share any of that. But he knew the guy had to have come along pretty soon after he and Kinley had been together in Vegas. And he didn't blame her for moving on. He'd pretty much told her it was that weekend and then goodbye.

But knowing she'd found someone else so quickly…well, it stung. It didn't matter that he knew he had no right to be upset or angry about it. He still was.

"Well… I'd ask her about him. He might be dead or he might be making child support payments. I'm sure Ethan will tell you the same thing. Legally, you should know what is going on."

Nate already had plans to talk to Ethan about it if things moved forward with him and Kinley. "Thanks, but what I really want to know is how to treat a kid. Can they talk when they are that young? I don't want to be awkward and freak the kid out."

King started laughing, which drew the attention of everyone else in their group, who demanded to know what was so funny. And of course King told them. Hunter came over to Nate, draping his arm around his brother's shoulder. "Why didn't you come to me? I know all about this thanks to Conner."

"Because you can be an ass when you think you know more than me," Nate said. Plus, he hadn't really been ready to talk about Kinley or anything else until he'd seen King talking to his son.

Nate wasn't getting domestic and he sure as hell wasn't sure he wanted to settle down, but he knew he was going to see Kinley again and that meant figuring out how to deal with her kid.

"Just give me some clue of how to deal with kids," Nate said. "Kinley has a two-year-old girl."

Hunter leaned in close. "It's easy, Nate. Kids are the world's greatest BS monitors, she'll know if you're being fake. Just relax and do your thing. She'll react better to you the more honest you are."

"Honest how?"

King leaned over. "Don't be fake nice to her because you want her to like you so you can hook up with her mom. That's what Hunter is saying. It's better to just leave the kid out of the picture if you can't get along with her. I dated a woman for a very short time who had a son Conner's age, but we just never connected and eventually the relationship ended."

Everyone else shared stories of dating, and though he wasn't a huge fan of sharing details of his personal life, Nate felt much better about meeting Kinley's daughter after talking about it with the guys. And he knew he was going to have to get some answers about the father of the baby at some point. But he figured it was better to do one thing at a time.

Kinley got home late from a long day and Pippa was waiting at the door for her. Today she wore her dark hair in a bob with purple-tinged ends. She had a small nose ring and always wore the brightest red lipstick that Kinley had ever seen. They were more like friends than boss and employee since they were only a few years apart in age, and more importantly they both were carrying around big secrets.

Pippa was on the run from her family in the UK. Having decided not to marry the wealthy aristocrat her family had selected for her, she'd escaped to Las Vegas, assumed a new identity and had been struggling to get work when Kinley met her. Kinley had been nine months pregnant, her water had broken and she'd been freaking out when Pippa had stepped up to help her.

A strong bond had been forged between the

women and working for Kinley enabled Pippa to stay off the grid and away from the private investigators that her family had looking for her.

"Penny is in a mood today. She's cranky and I think she might be getting in one of her molars. I need a drink and a break."

"You've got it. I could use some Mommy and Penny time," Kinley said. "Are you going out?"

"Not likely," Pippa said. "I spotted a guy at the airport who I thought might be following me, and I'm pretty sure I saw him at the park when Penny was playing today. I wonder if I've been caught."

Kinley hugged her friend. "Let me see Penny and then we'll figure this out. Go and get yourself some wine and sit by the pool."

"Thanks, Kin."

"No problem," Kinley said. It was nice to have someone else's problems to worry about instead of just her own. Pippa had lived with them since Penny was born and Kinley considered her a heart sister.

She went down the hall to Penny's bedroom, and as soon as she stepped inside she saw what Pippa had meant. All of Penny's stuffed animals and dolls were lined up facing the wall.

"Hey, sweet girl," Kinley said as she walked into the room. "What's going on here?"

"Hi, Mama," Penny said. "Someone was bad."

"Want to tell me about it?" Kinley asked as she

came into the room and sat down next to Penny. Kinley dropped a kiss on the top of her daughter's head, and as she did so she noticed that there were marks on the wall in front of Penny's toys. Kinley leaned in for a closer look and realized it was lipstick.

"Did you write on the wall with lipstick?" she asked.

Penny shook her head back and forth. "Not me. But one of them."

Kinley had spoken with her daughter about lying before. Every time Penny got in trouble there was usually a stuffed animal to blame. "Who do you think did it?"

"Mr. Beans," she said. The large fluffy bunny rabbit was dressed in overalls that had jelly beans on it. He was the closest to the lipstick stains on the wall, and as Kinley leaned over she noticed that it looked as if Mr. Beans had tried putting the lipstick on himself. And then she groaned when she realized it was the expensive tube of Marc Jacobs lipstick that she'd splurged on last month.

"I think someone had to help Mr. Beans," Kinley said to Penny. "Someone who knows where Mama keeps her lipstick. And who may have tried one on this morning when Mama was getting ready."

Penny stared up at her with those wide gray-blue

eyes of hers. Kinley kept her stare level until finally Penny ducked her head. "It was me."

Kinley put her finger under her daughter's chin. "I know. How did it happen?"

"During nap time," Penny said.

Kinley knew that Penny slept in Kinley's bed during nap time because she liked to be closer to her. Pippa usually worked on an anonymous blog she wrote that focused on commentary on high-end fashion and beauty during that time.

"So you finished up your nap and decided to do Mr. Beans's makeup?" Kinley asked.

"He was having a down day. Lipstick always cheers you up," Penny said.

"It sure does. But you have to ask and you need supervision to use it," Kinley said. "Come on, let's go get our cleaning supplies. And I think you owe Pippa an apology. She said you were cranky."

Penny got to her feet and Kinley led the way back to the kitchen. When they got there, Penny went over to the screen door, which was closed, and put her face against it. "I'm sorry, Pippa."

Pippa looked over from her spot on the pool deck and smiled at Penny. "It's all right, imp. We all have bad days."

Penny came back over and together they attempted to clean the lipstick off the wall. As they were working, Kinley realized just how busy she'd been with her job lately, mostly to avoid seeing Nate, and that she hadn't been spending as much time with her daughter as she'd like. So she spent the rest of the night playing with Penny and getting in as much good mommy time as she could.

Kinley knew whatever happened in her life, she couldn't let her daughter suffer for it. Penny needed her mom. Kinley had always promised herself that she'd put her child first and not her job, but it felt like she was falling into the same habits her parents had, which worried her, because Nate was a workaholic as well. But she remembered her own parents and how each of them had given her something different. She'd always thought she was enough for Penny, but now that Nate was back in her life, she wanted Penny to know her dad. And Penny deserved two parents who were there for her all the time.

Nine

Nate took an early morning flight back from LA and drove himself home from Houston. He stopped at a coffee shop on Main Street, groaning when he realized the line was long and he probably should have gone to his office, but then he caught a glimpse of Kinley's red hair pulled back in a ponytail. She was toward the front of the line. He opened the door and walked inside, doffing his Stetson and putting his sunglasses on top of his head. He skimmed his gaze down her back, remembering how much he missed her when he noticed she held a little girl's hand.

Her daughter.

He almost turned around and walked out the door and away from her. But when he'd been in Los Angeles, he'd thought of Kinley the entire time. Not just hot, sexy daydreams, which could be justified, but other dreams where he held her in his arms all night, and even better still, where he was sitting and talking to her. He remembered their dinner conversation and wanted to spend more time with her.

He liked the woman she was and needed to continue getting to know her. And despite the fact that he wasn't anyone's first choice when it came to being a parent, he was very good at maneuvering around circumstances and making things work. He could do this.

He remembered what King had said about kids being BS meters and decided he'd just be himself. But just then, Kinley looked over her shoulder at him and then looked down at her daughter. The little girl wore a pair of jeans and a flowery shirt and had her hair in a ponytail similar to Kinley's. There were several customers between them in the line and the entire time the line moved, even while making small talk with men he knew from high school or business, Nate kept his eyes on Kinley.

His attention stayed on Kinley and he wondered as he watched her. Who was the man who'd convinced her to have a child with him? Then it hit him that the baby might have been accidental. Was that why the father wasn't in the picture?

He hated to think of the kind of man who would have abandoned Kinley when she'd been pregnant. That wasn't a real man, he thought.

She ordered her drinks and her daughter skipped away from the counter over to a table in the corner, where a woman with purple-striped hair was waiting. Kinley took their tray and came over to the table and he noticed that she leaned in and talked to the other woman. Then she scooped her daughter up and gave her a hug and kiss before shouldering her large workbag and walking out of the coffee shop.

Nate was next in line. He ordered his drink and then quickly followed Kinley outside. She hadn't gone too far; in fact, she was leaning against his pickup truck when he walked up to it.

"Hiya, Nate," she said. "I wanted a chance to apologize for the other night."

"There's nothing to apologize for. I meant to call you and see if you wanted to go on another date," he said. "But I was in LA and I heard you were out of town."

"From Hunter?" she asked.

"Yeah. Though it is hard to keep secrets in this town," he said.

Kinley turned away, opened her bag and began searching for something. She found her sunglasses and put them on. "Yes, it is. I haven't dated at all since I had Penny, and I think I might have been a little awkward when I told you about her. I'd like another chance, so I was wondering if you wanted to join me for dinner tonight…at my place. My daughter will be there, too."

Kinley sounded nervous and unsure of herself. Not at all like the Kinley he knew. He realized that his reaction to her daughter had probably spooked her a bit. It made him realize that whatever had happened with the man who had come after him had shaken and changed her. Maybe as much as having a daughter on her own.

"I'd love to. But I can't tonight. I was gone for four days and I have a board dinner tonight."

"Of course. It's an open invitation. Just text me when you have some free time in your schedule," she said. She glanced at her watch. "I have to run. Have a good one."

She turned before he could say anything else, and he almost let her walk away, except he was a Caruthers. He caught up with her in two steps and caught her wrist, stopping her.

"Nate?"

"Sorry. I forgot to say that I missed you and that I'm sorry I wasn't better prepared to hear that you had a kid. It shook me, but it didn't change the way I feel about you, Kin," he said.

"How do you feel about me?" she asked.

"I want to get to know you better. I want a chance to see if that weekend we spent together was just a fluke or if we have something solid," he said. "Will you take a chance on that?"

She bit her lower lip and then pushed her sunglasses up with her free hand. "I'd like that, but we need to talk a little more. There is something I have to tell you."

"Go on then, girl," he said.

She glanced around as early morning commuters streamed past them on the sidewalk, and she shook her head. "Not here. Let me know when you're free and we can talk."

He wasn't sure what it was that she had to say that had her so spooked. He let her hand drop and then nodded and walked back to his truck without a backward glance. He hoped she was watching him leave, but he couldn't confirm it. *Wouldn't*.

He was pretty sure that she wanted him with the same intensity that he wanted her, but there was unfinished business in her mind. He only hoped it wasn't her trying to get even for the callous way he'd treated her almost three years ago.

Kinley's heart was racing like a prize thoroughbred nearing the finish line at the Kentucky Derby as Nate turned and walked away from her. She waited until he got in his truck and took a deep breath. This was getting more and more complicated.

It reminded her of something her mom used to say: "Don't start lying unless you want to keep doing it for the rest of your life." Kinley wished she'd remembered it sooner. Jacs had said that everything would work out, and Kinley knew that she absolutely couldn't let any more time go by before she told him. But blurting it out on the sidewalk while everyone was heading toward work wasn't the right thing to do.

She wasn't exactly sure how Nate was going to react when he learned that he was Penny's father, but she was pretty sure he wasn't going to be calm and collected. He was a man of passions and, if town gossip was to be believed, a quick temper.

She was sweating. Not from the heat, though the temperature in southern Texas was rising already on this hot June morning. It was from her own fears.

"Mama!"

She turned to see Pippa and Penny walking toward her, and tears stung the back of her eyes as she looked at her daughter. She'd only ever wanted what was best for her, and now she was afraid, really afraid that she might have made the wrong decision when she'd let Nate push her aside when she'd called.

Now she could think of a bunch of scenarios where maybe she could have flown to Texas or written him a note, but at the time, his words had been blunt and hurtful. But now he definitely wasn't the same man he'd been three years ago. For one thing he was hanging around her and there was a sense of real commitment in him. Still, she worried that the man he was today wasn't going to understand her motivations for her keeping Penny secret.

Pippa took one look at her face as she got closer and picked Penny up in her arms.

"Are you okay?"

"Yes. Sorry. I'm just trying to figure out how to do what I have to do, and it keeps getting harder."

Pippa nodded. "Want me to do it?"

Kinley smiled at her friend. "It would be easier for me but I'm pretty sure that it would only make it worse."

"Make what worse, Mama?" Penny asked.

"Just something I have to do, sweet girl," Kinley said, reaching over and stroking the back of Penny's head. Her daughter shifted and reached for her and Kinley took her from Pippa, holding her close. Penny put her little arms around Kinley and hugged her, giving her a sloppy kiss on the chin. Kinley felt a little bit of peace stealing through her.

She'd make it right for Nate once she told him and found out how much he wanted to be in Pen-

ny's life. He might not want to, she realized. And
that made her sad. Really sad. Because she wanted
the man she kept getting glimpses of to be the kind
that would want his own child.

"Would you like to come to work with me today?"
she asked Penny.

"Yes! Pippa can come, too," Penny said.

"I can?" Pippa asked. "Maybe I need a break
from you, imp."

"Nah, you love me."

"I do," Pippa said as Kinley put Penny down.

They all started walking up the street toward
her offices. She and Pippa each held one of Penny's
hands. Then they counted to three and swung her
between them. And Kinley realized as they walked
that of all the regrets she had about Penny, she never
had any doubts she'd provided a good, solid home
for her daughter. Pippa was like an aunt to Penny
and the three of them were close. She wondered how
Nate would fit in with the dynamic, but she refused
to worry about it any more. She would tell him.

He said he had a meeting tonight. She should text
him and push him to get a time for dinner scheduled. She made up her mind to do it as soon as she
had a free moment at work.

But when they got to her office, Meredith, the
bride from Dallas, was waiting in her Porsche
Cayenne in the parking lot. She got out as soon as

she saw Kinley walking up. She pushed her sunglasses up on her head, and Kinley saw that the other woman had been crying. Her makeup had run, and she looked like she was about to lose it.

"Pippa, can you take Penny inside and let her play in my office?" Kinley said, handing her key ring to Pippa. "Mama will be in soon."

She kissed Penny as Pippa took her toward the building.

"Meredith, are you okay?"

"No. Everything is a complete mess. Someone else has my dress," Meredith said.

Kinley didn't think that was possible, since Meredith had picked out every item that would go on her dress, but she put her arm around Meredith and led her into the office, which Pippa had already opened up. Kinley got Meredith seated and talking about her concerns.

They made a video call to the designer in Beverly Hills to talk about the changes Meredith wanted. She had confessed to Kinley that the bride whose dress was similar to hers was her fiancé's former girlfriend.

It took Kinley most of the day to get her calmed down. Six hours later, Meredith was in a hotel room in the Cole's Hill Grand Hotel and her fiancé was on his way down from Dallas to join her. But the crisis was averted.

She finally had time to text Nate. She told him they needed to talk.

She saw that the text was delivered and kept checking her phone all night, but there was no response.

Nate went to the Five Families Country Club after he finished the board meeting. It was close to midnight by the time he finally had a moment to think. He'd had two whiskeys with beer chasers so he knew his responses were alcohol driven. He was in the mood to do something to prove that Kinley didn't have the power over him that he knew she did. So when Derek showed up straight from a late-night emergency surgery with that wild look in his eyes, Nate knew that his brother needed him, and maybe he needed Derek, too.

Reprieve, he thought. He would text her in the morning when he was less likely to say something rash.

Early on, right after Derek had become a surgeon and he'd lost his first patient, Nate had been the one to spend all night drinking with his brother until he could talk about it.

Derek had started college when he was fifteen and had graduated from medical school at twenty-one. He was one of the youngest in his field but one of the brightest.

Then he'd held him until he fell asleep. There were times when Nate knew exactly what someone needed from him. And as the oldest Caruthers, he usually was pretty good about figuring out what his brothers needed. He'd done the same thing for Hunter when he'd first been released from police questioning in the Frat House Murder.

"Rough night?"

"I don't want to talk about it," Derek said.

"Drinking, fighting or pool?" Nate asked.

"Drinking and pool. Maybe if you cheat, some fighting," Derek said.

"You go rack 'em up. I'll grab the drinks," Nate said.

Derek walked past him into the game room at the club. It had been built in a Spanish style with large, sweeping arches and lots of rooms for events, games and televisions for game day. There were three restaurants: one upscale, one with counter service and one that women really seemed to like because they served an afternoon tea and brunch. In the summer kids from Cole's Hill's Five Families neighborhood could use their parents' accounts to charge food and play games. It had been like a second home to the Carutherses growing up, since their dad was a descendant of the Five Families.

Nate signaled one of the waitresses and told her to get him a bottle of Jack and two glasses and bring it to the Caruthlerses' room. He walked into the room to find Derek leaning forward with his hands on the bumper of the pool table. He cleared his throat so Derek would know he wasn't alone.

Derek straightened up, turning to look at Nate as he entered. His thick blond hair was rumpled, as if he'd spent a lot of time running his hands through it. Derek liked to wear suits, but he'd loosened his tie, taken off the jacket and rolled his sleeves up. Nate went to the paneled wall and took down two cue sticks.

He handed one to Derek just as Carly, the waitress, brought in the bottle and glasses.

"Thanks, Carly."

"No problem. I'm off in twenty minutes if you want some company," she said.

He thought about it for a split second but knew that the last thing he wanted was to complicate things with Kinley any more than they already were. He shook his head. "Not tonight."

She looked disappointed but nodded and then disappeared. As soon as the door closed, Derek arched one eyebrow at him. "Sorry to cut in on your action."

"You're not."

"I'm not?" Derek asked. "You got a woman now?"

"I've been sort of seeing Kinley," Nate said. "You can shoot first."

"Wait a minute. Marcus's daughter? That Kinley?"

"Yeah," Nate said. "But we're not in here because of her. You are the one who—"

"Needs a distraction," Derek said. "And listening to you try to get out of talking about her is pretty damned amusing."

"I haven't had near enough to drink to be amusing," Nate said.

"So there's a chance you could provide entertainment later," Derek said, leaning over the table to break.

They played pool until three in the morning and eventually ended up just sitting on the floor with the bottle of Jack between them and talking.

"Did you lose a patient?" Nate finally felt like it was the right time to ask.

"Yeah. I was on call. An accident out on the highway. I thought I had him, and I did for a short while and then…" Derek poured more than two fingers of liquor into his highball glass and swallowed it, putting his head back against the paneled wall. He drew his knee up and rested his hand on it.

"What's going on with Kinley?" Derek asked. "She's not your type."

"You couldn't be more wrong," Nate told him.

"Truly?" Derek asked, arching one brow. His eyes were bloodshot—he'd probably had enough to drink.

"Yeah. She's different," Nate said. He took another swallow from his glass and realized it was empty, so he poured himself another one. He thought about how Kinley for him was like those photos his mom loved so much, where everyone in the background was in black-and-white and then in the forefront there would be an image or a person in color.

Kinley was in full-blown color and other women were starting to fade to black-and-white. But he knew better than to say that out loud. Despite the fact that Derek had drunk more than he had, Nate knew his brother would recall every moment of the evening. It had happened before.

"Good. I always thought you should settle down before Hunter," Derek said.

"Why the hell?"

"Oldest and all that. It won't be long before you start losing your hair like Dad and maybe getting a beer belly," Derek said.

"You're an ass," Nate said. Their father still had a full head of hair and didn't have a belly.

"I am," Derek said. "An ass who can't save everyone."

Nate reached over and draped his arm around his brother's shoulders. "No one can save everyone. Did you make any mistakes?"

"No. I've been over it again and again in my

head. I tried to figure out if it would have mattered if the ambulance had gotten to us five minutes sooner or if I had shaved off a few minutes when I scrubbed up... I just don't know what else I could have done."

"Life is like that, D. Sometimes we have to accept that things are out of our control."

"I can't. I'm supposed to be able to save everyone," he said. "Natey, don't tell anyone else I can't."

"I won't, D," he said to his brother. "I promise."

He kept his arm around Derek and thought about the mistakes he'd made with Kinley and knew it was past time he made up for them. He didn't need alcohol to show him what he wanted to say. He just needed honesty, and sometimes that was the hardest thing to find.

Ten

Nate didn't dwell too deeply on the fact that he was driving around the Five Families neighborhood looking for Kinley's rented house early the next evening. He hadn't had to be Sherlock Holmes to get the address—a call to Hunter had been sufficient—and now he was sitting in front of her place, wondering if she'd let him in if he knocked on her door.

He also wondered what time a two-year-old kid went to bed. He put his head forward on the steering wheel. It wasn't like him to be indecisive.

But the kid had thrown a monkey wrench in his plans.

Rekindling things with Kinley was one thing.

He had been fairly confident that a summer affair would suit them both. But not now.

He saw the front porch light come on and the curtains move in the front window. Now he looked like a creeper sitting out here. He opened the door to the cab of his truck and hopped down, walking up the front path toward the door.

He hit the doorbell and stood back to wait. He wasn't standing there long before it swung open and he found himself staring into Kinley's warm brown eyes. She wasn't wearing any makeup and had her hair pulled back in a ponytail, with only a light fall of bangs hanging down on her forehead. She had on a pair of leggings and a sleeveless T-shirt that fell to her thighs. Her feet were bare and next to her was a little girl in a matching outfit with the same red hair. But her eyes were blue. A beautiful light blue that seemed to sparkle.

"Hello, cowboy," the child said.

"Hello," he replied, stooping down so he was on eye level with her. She smiled at him, her grin just as sweet as Kinley's. "I'm Nate."

"I'm Penny," she said, holding out her hand.

He shook it carefully before standing up. "Sorry to drop by without notice," he said. "Work has been keeping both of us busy, but I wanted to see you."

"Work has been crazy lately. What did you want?" she asked.

Penny kept staring up at him. He wondered what it was that she was staring at, so he took off his Stetson and held it out to her in case it was his hat.

She started to reach for it, but Kinley stopped her. "What are you doing here, Nate?"

"I missed you. I regret the way things ended the other night, so I thought I'd stop by and apologize—damn—I mean darn. I do that a lot with you," he said. It was true. She seemed to be the one woman in the world who could rattle him with little effort.

"I think we both are to blame for the other night," she said. "We are baking cookies. Would you like to come in and help us?"

He looked down at Penny, who was smiling and nodding up at him. "Mama is making horsey cookies."

"I'd love to help," Nate said.

Penny reached for his hat again, and he let her have it. She plopped it on her head and it fell down to cover her eyes, but she pushed it up so she could see before she turned and ran up the hall.

She was charming; he had the feeling that she got away with a lot. He knew that he'd easily say yes to anything she asked him if she smiled up at him with that gap-toothed grin of hers.

He stepped inside the foyer and closed the door behind him. The floor was Spanish tile and the ceilings were high and vaulted. As Kinley turned and he followed her, he noticed that despite the fact that she would only be in Cole's Hill for six months, she'd hung pictures on the wall.

He knew they were hers, because all of them were of her daughter, save for one of Kinley with her parents at her high school graduation. When he entered the kitchen he saw it was spacious and there was a large island in the middle with a sturdy-looking wooden step next to one side of the counter and cookie sheets as well as a bowl of dough in the middle.

Penny was nowhere to be seen. The kitchen was modern and sleek, and he noticed that there were two double ovens that were both preheating.

"How many cookies are you making?" he asked.

"Two dozen. It's Penny's turn to bring the snack in at her day care tomorrow," Kinley said.

Nate was having a time trying to reconcile the two versions of Kinley. She was very domestic now, which he hadn't expected or truly caught a glimpse of before this.

"Where's your daughter?" he asked.

"Over here," she called, as she reentered the room on a broomstick horse that made a clip-clopping sound as she rode it around the kitchen. "I'm a real cowgirl."

"Yes, you are," Kinley said. "But it's time to put

Buttercup back in her stable so we can finish making our cookies."

"'Kay," the little girl said.

"She has a stable?"

"We made one in her room out of one of the moving boxes. She's horse crazy," Kinley said a bit nervously. "Dad has been showing her the horses on the Rockin' C every time they have a video chat."

"Did he tell you that your mama used to be a cowgirl?" Nate asked.

"Yup. And he showed me her bucks."

"Bucks?" Nate asked, looking at Kinley.

"My buckles from the rodeos I competed in," she said.

He remembered another girl who had been horse crazy. And it made him realize that something inside him was changing. He couldn't say why, but he didn't want to stay here in this warm kitchen with Kinley and Penny. The two girls talked and laughed, and he felt out of his element. But just like when he'd first stepped into the boardroom to take over his father's position, he also felt something like excitement in the pit of his stomach.

Kinley was surprised to see Nate in her home, being so charmingly awkward around Penny. When he showed up here tonight she'd seen it as fate's way of forcing her to talk to him about his daughter. And this was a chance she couldn't let slip by again. She took her iPhone out when they were both concentrating on the cookies and snapped a few pictures of the two of them together.

A heavy weight was on her heart, and she knew that the time had come. No more delays or excuses. It was harder this time than it had been after their recent times together, because tonight she could see the softer side of Nate. And she knew that once he learned Penny was his, he wasn't easily going to forgive Kinley for not telling him.

Part of why Nate had softened up was because their daughter was being very sweet with him tonight. Penny always had been a bit of a flirt with men. Pippa had said it might be due to the fact that she didn't have a father.

But she did have one.

And he was here now.

He was definitely out of his element. He had worn his Stetson, faded jeans and a designer shirt with leather loafers. He was not exactly full-on cowboy tonight, but he was quintessentially Nate. He was a mix of rancher, businessman and jet-setting playboy. And he was sitting in the breakfast nook next to Penny, helping her decorate horse-shaped sugar cookies. He was patient as she directed him on the different colors and patterns he should put on each horse.

"Mama, what did your horse look like growing up?" Penny asked.

"She had a paint," Nate said. "I remember what it looked like."

"You knew her?" Penny asked.

"Yes, I did. Your grandfather works for me," he said.

Penny put her tiny hand on Nate's shoulder and leaned around him to look over at Kinley, who was standing by the sink.

"Pop-Pop," Kinley said.

"Oh. So all the horsies belong to you?"

"Some of them, but not all. Do you want to come and see the horses?"

"Yes. Mama, did you hear that?"

"I did," Kinley said. But she wasn't too sure the invitation would stand after she and Nate spoke later this evening. She wasn't going to let him leave without telling him the truth. "We will figure out a time for a visit. Pop-Pop already wants us to come out there."

"Just let me know," Nate said. "I think that's the last cookie. What do we do now?"

Penny clambered over his lap and then turned around on the bench to slide down feetfirst. "This."

She reached for the tray with her tiny, chubby hands, holding it very carefully. Kinley was already on her way to the table as Penny tipped it to lift it.

Nate reached underneath the tray and steadied it for her until she was on her feet. Then he helped her readjust her hold.

Penny walked over to her, carrying the tray, and Kinley blinked as she realized for the first time what she'd unintentionally stolen from Nate. He might have said he didn't want to hear from her again, but he had missed out on fatherhood, which wasn't fair.

Kinley hurried over to take the cookies from Penny. "Why don't you show Nate where the bathroom is and wash up?"

"'Kay. Come on, Nate," she said, taking his hand.

Nate didn't hesitate, just took her hand in his and followed her down the hall. Kinley grabbed her phone and texted Pippa, who was in town doing some grocery shopping. She wanted to warn her before she came home. She was definitely going to go to a special kind of hell if she didn't finally tell Nate her secret. And she was going to do it tonight. But she didn't want Pippa to walk in on them fighting if he got angry.

Kinley began typing.

Nate's here. Penny already likes him. I'm so scared.

The response was immediate.

You got this, girl. Want me to come and get Penny?

I think it might be better if I put her to bed with Nate and then tell him. He seems to like her.

Of course he likes her. Okay, want me to stay in town?

Yeah, for now. I don't know how long it will take to tell him.

I'll go to a movie. Text me when it's safe to come home. I'll get groceries tomorrow.

Thanks, Pip. Wish me luck.

She closed the text app on her phone as she heard Nate and Penny coming back down the hall.

Penny tried to climb up on one of the breakfast bar chairs and Nate scooped her up in his arms and turned to Kinley. He and their daughter both had the same expression on their faces, and her heart broke. It just broke right open, because she wasn't sure what was going to happen when she told Nate. But she knew things were never going to be the same, and she was pretty sure Nate was never going to look at her with that happy expression in his eyes again.

"What do we do now?" he asked.

"We get to eat 'em," Penny said, turning her head toward Nate's. She noticed his five o'clock shadow and lifted her hand to his face. "You're prickly."

"Not all the time," he said, smiling at her. "You're sweet."

"Not all the time," she said back to him. "Sometimes I'm naughty."

Kinley rolled her eyes. "Okay, missy, that's enough. You can put her down on the chair."

"I like him, Mama."

Kinley took a deep breath and let it out. "I do, too."

Nate had never expected to be a part of a bedtime ritual. But helping with Penny reminded him a lot of when his brothers were younger. By the time Nate was ten, his mom had been tired from riding herd on him and his brothers every day and had put Nate in charge of bedtime. That meant he'd supervised everyone getting into their PJs and brushing and flossing their teeth. Then they'd all go into their parents' bedroom and climb up on their big bed for a story. When they were done, they'd kiss their parents good-night and head to bed. Nate always turned off the lights in his brothers' rooms before going to his own.

And then they stayed in their rooms until it was time to get up in the morning.

Not so with Penny.

"I'm thirssy," Penny said the first time she'd come back into the living room, where Kinley had suggested they sit down.

Kinley got up and poured her a glass of water and put her back in bed, then came out and sat down next to him again.

"Sorry about that," Kinley said. "Usually she goes right to sleep, but I think she's afraid she's missing out on talking to a real cowboy."

"It's okay. Wait until you take her out to the ranch. She'll go nuts," Nate said. He was slightly surprised that Kinley hadn't already taken her out there, except on Memorial Day. Given the fact that her daughter was clearly horse crazy and her grandfather was there, it seemed like they'd be visiting more often. "Why haven't you brought her out before this?"

"Actually—

"I'm scared. Something's under my bed," Penny said again from the hallway.

"Penelope Grace, stop getting out of bed," Kinley said in a very stern voice.

"But Mama," Penny said.

Kinley got up and scooped her daughter into her arms and went down the hall again. This time she was there for about fifteen minutes, so Nate put on ESPN and noticed they were rerunning a one-hour special they'd made about King and Hunter being cleared of all suspicion in the Frat House Murder. As happy as he was that his brother had been cleared, Nate definitely didn't want to watch that, so he flipped channels until he found an NBA play-off game and then settled back to wait.

He had enjoyed spending the evening with Kinley and her daughter. It was so different than what he'd expected, but the longer he'd been in the house the more natural it was to him to see Penny and Kinley together. It had seemed at first as if Kinley was different here, but she was the same way with her daughter as she was with everyone else. Only more relaxed.

She laughed more easily, and she watched her daughter constantly with love in her gaze and more than a little bit of pride. He could easily see himself fitting into their lives, but the one thing he wasn't sure about was his own track record with long-term relationships.

His mom had always said when the right girl came along he'd know it.

Was Kinley that right girl?

He was beginning to think she might be.

"Okay. Sorry about that. I think she is going to stay put now," Kinley said.

"I know I would. You sounded very stern," Nate said.

Kinley shook her head. "Sometimes I have to be firm. Otherwise she thinks I'm not serious."

"I'm beginning to see that all that charm she was showing me earlier could be hard to resist," Nate said. "I wanted to ask you about her father. I'm sorry I didn't the other night."

Kinley nodded. "We both didn't handle things very well. I wanted to talk to you about that very same thing."

"Good. I wasn't feeding you a line the other day in town. I do want us to date. And I know Penny is part of the package. She's too cute for words."

Kinley crossed her legs underneath her body and then wrapped her arms around her waist as she leaned forward. "She is adorable. I feel so lucky to have her."

"You are," he said. "What kind of jerk wouldn't want his own kid?"

She took a deep breath. "Um…it's sort of complicated, and once you hear the story, please understand I did the best I could."

"Okay," he said. "I'm not going to judge you, Kinley. I know you're a sweet girl, and the way I rejected you on the phone must have sent you into a tailspin. I'm not judging you for hooking up with someone else after our weekend."

Kinley suddenly stood up and walked away from the couch toward the entertainment center and then turned to face him again. Her face was ashen, and she put her hands on her hips then let them drop to her sides.

"There wasn't anyone else, Nate. There was only you. When I called you, it was to tell you I was pregnant. I didn't know what else to do after you said what you did, and honestly, I never thought I'd see you again. The other night when I mentioned Penny's age, I just assumed you'd figure out you were the dad. That was my bad, but you are Penny's father. There wasn't anyone after you. Just you."

He stared at her, trying to process the torrent of words coming from her mouth but he'd stopped listening after she'd said he was Penny's father.

He was a father.

A father.

Penny was his daughter.

He stood up and looked at Kinley. He watched her shrink back from him—not that he'd ever hurt her, but he was pissed and he knew it showed. Pissed at her for telling him now and not telling him then. Pissed at himself for not figuring it out earlier. Just good and pissed.

He turned away from her and walked down the hall to Penny's bedroom and stood there in the doorway, watching her sleep with a stuffed bunny tucked under arm in the illumination of her night-light.

His daughter.

Eleven

Kinley watched Nate watching Penny and waited. While she felt guilty about not telling him before they'd recently slept together again, she didn't regret not telling him before she came to Texas. Even now as they were starting to get to know each other, she still wasn't sure exactly what he was going to want from her.

How involved would he want to be in Penny's life? She suspected his parents were going to be very excited to have a grandchild, but what about Nate? And where did that leave Kinley?

She'd told him because she'd started to care for him again. Which was a total lie, she thought as she realized she'd never really stopped caring for him. It was like that stupid, secret fantasy from her childhood when she'd seen the other kids at school with their perfect nuclear families and longed for that for herself.

He turned to face her, and the raw emotion on his face made her want to comfort him. She walked closer to him, intent on hugging him, but he held his hand up and shook his head. He stalked past her in the hall, back toward the living room.

She checked on Penny and noticed her daughter was sleeping peacefully with Mr. Beans tucked up against her side. Her daughter was completely unaware of the storm that was raging in the house.

Kinley closed the door, leaving it slightly ajar, before going back into the living room. It was empty, but she followed the sound of the china cabinet's doors opening and closing into the dining room, where she found Nate with a bottle of Glenlivet that she and Pippa drank occasionally.

Nate had a squat glass in one hand and had poured several fingers of scotch into it.

"So... I think we need to talk," Kinley said. She had one arm around her waist but remembered an article that Jacs had made her read about how the posture made a person seem defensive.

But she was sort of defensive. She'd done the best she could.

"I'm sorry I didn't tell you before," she said. "But you weren't exactly listening to anything I had to say on the phone."

"I know," he said, grinding the words out between swallows. "Give me a few minutes, Kinley, or I might say something I'll regret."

She nodded and left him alone in her dining room with the scotch and went into the kitchen to clean up the counters. They were already spotless but a little extra polish wouldn't hurt.

"Does your father know I'm Penny's dad?" Nate asked, startling her as he entered the kitchen.

She pivoted to face him and saw him leaning against the arch that led to the dining room. He held the bottle loosely in one hand and the glass in the other.

"No. I told him that the father isn't in the picture," she said.

His eyes narrowed. "Did you say I didn't want her?"

"No. I didn't tell him it was you. I did tell him about the phone call and hanging up on me, but not that it was you. Do you remember that? How I was trying to talk to you and you said we both had fun, but it was over and we should go back to our normal lives?" she asked. She was trying to be calm and let him work through things, but she wasn't going to allow him to try to reframe the past. The truth was she'd tried to tell him, and he hadn't wanted to hear anything she had to say.

"I do remember that. I'm trying to make myself feel better for missing out on two years of my daughter's life, but there is nothing that can change that, is there?"

"Not really," she said. "I have tried to think of a better way that I could have handled things, but honestly I was alone and scared and didn't want Dad to lose his job, so I stayed in Vegas and did the best I could."

Nate put the bottle and glass on the countertop and walked over to her. He stopped when there were a few feet of space separating them and then tipped his head to the side. "Did you hate me?"

"A little bit," she admitted. "But mainly I was mad at myself for not being more careful. All of those feelings went away the minute Penny was born and I held her in my arms. And then, Nate, even though I believed I'd never see you again, I was grateful to you for giving her to me. She's made my life so much richer and forced me to grow up."

He stared at her and didn't say anything else for a long time. Kinley wondered what he was thinking. But now that she was talking about Penny, all her anger had evaporated. And she knew that they needed to make some plans...if he wanted to be involved in Penny's life.

She licked her suddenly dry lips, trying to figure out how to ask him. What if he said no? He might need time. She'd had nine months to get used to the idea of being a mom—well, more like seven, since she'd been in denial after she'd first found out.

"What do you want to do next?" she asked.

"About what?"

"Penny," she said. "Do you want to be her father? Do you want to be in her life? Or do you want to keep things as they are?"

He cursed and looked down at the floor. "Boy, you know how to kick a man when he's down."

Kinley stared at him. "What do you mean?"

"Just that you must think I'm some kind of scumbag to not want my daughter to know I'm her father. What kind of man do you think I am?"

Kinley looked at him and answered honestly. "I have no idea. We've had sex and talked a few times, but we don't know each other, Nate. I don't know what is in your heart or in your mind when it comes to raising a family."

This night just kept getting better and better, Nate realized. If he'd needed a stark reality check, then Penny and Kinley had definitely provided him with one. He'd always thought of himself as a protector and told himself he'd left no damage behind when he moved on from his relationships, but now he saw that might not have been true.

"I want my daughter. I will be claiming her and I will be raising her," Nate said. "In fact, I've already texted Ethan, and he's going to start working on the papers needed for me to officially be named as her father. In my heart and mind is that sweet little girl who has been living without me."

Kinley let out a long breath. "I'm glad to hear that. I think kids need both parents. I am happy to have my attorney look at whatever papers Ethan draws up. We can have your name added to her birth certificate in Nevada, and then we can work on some sort of visitation for you."

"Visitation? I'm going to be her father, Kinley. I'm not going to be one of those dads that drifts in and out of his kid's life. We are going to figure out a way to share custody and make sure that Penny has the best damned childhood ever."

Nate already had a few ideas of things he was going to have to change. In fact, drinking was probably one of them. And he lived equally between the ranch house and his penthouse here in town, but Kinley would probably prefer to live on the ranch, so Nate could easily work from there until Penny was older and started school.

"We can discuss it, but for right now you are going to have to transition into her life. You and I can come up with whatever plan we think is best for her, but the truth is, change is hard on kids. I have a nanny who watches Penny while I work," Kinley said. She moved to a drawer in the kitchen and opened it, taking out a pen and pad. "Do you want to hash this out tonight or wait and do it tomorrow?"

Tonight. But he wasn't thinking clearly. He was still mad and trying to process that he had a daughter. He was afraid he was going to react instead of think things through. Ethan was one of the best lawyers in the country, so Nate had no doubt his brother would get him whatever Nate asked for. But once he spoke to his brother, he was going to have to tell his mom and dad he had a kid.

"I have to tell my parents," he said. It hit him that his mom was going to be over the moon to find out she had a granddaughter. She'd always wanted a little girl, and he felt a spark of anger toward Kinley and himself for keeping Penny a secret for so long.

"I know. I have to tell my dad," she said. "This is complicated."

A twinge of guilt and embarrassment went through Nate. He had always respected Marcus and thought that Marcus had grown to respect the man Nate had become, but he knew this would change things. He'd made a clean break with Kinley because he hadn't wanted complications almost three years ago, and now he had more snags than he'd ever guessed he could have.

A daughter.

Nothing had been farther from his mind before this night. He'd thought about dating a woman with a kid, not about being a father himself. But tonight when he'd sat on that bench in the kitchen nook with Penny, he'd fallen for her charm. Nate had thought it was because she was Kinley's daughter, but now he was going to put it down to some sort of latent paternal instinct.

"It is…they are going to expect me to marry you," Nate said.

"Marry you? We aren't living in the 1890s. This is the twenty-first century. Parents don't have to be married."

"In Cole's Hill they do. Your dad isn't going to be happy knowing I knocked you up and told you to get lost," Nate said. "Either I make this right—the way our parents would expect me to—or we have to come up with some sort of better story than the truth."

"No," she said, shaking her head. "No more lies. And we can't just marry. We don't even know each other and I'm not sure if we'd even get along."

"We get along in bed," he said.

"There's more to life than that," she said. "I… I can't marry you just because of our daughter."

Nate could see that Kinley was going to be stubborn about this. He wanted to understand her reasons, but now that the thought had entered his mind, he knew he wasn't going to be happy with anything less than having Penny and Kinley both in his life permanently. "Why not?"

She chewed her lower lip and wrapped her arms around her waist again, then dropped them and put her hands on the countertop behind her. The action thrust her breasts forward, and for the first time since she'd dropped her bombshell he saw Kinley as the woman who had him tied in knots and not as the woman who'd kept a huge secret from him.

"I'm waiting," he said.

"My parents married because of me. And they didn't get along and hated each other. They were miserable, and my mom took a job that kept her away from my dad. I always wanted something better for Penny."

Nate wanted the best for Penny, too. He doubted that he and Kinley would end up resenting each other, but if she needed time maybe he'd give it to her—at least in terms of getting married. Penny was going to know she had a father now.

Kinley realized that things were no longer in her control. Nate was talking about marriage…marriage! There was no way that was happening. She'd watched her mom blossom as soon as she'd divorced

Marcus and left Texas. And to be honest, Kinley might have thought it would be nice to have that perfect image of a family, but in reality she wasn't too sure she could live with someone else.

There was Pippa, but they were both pretty independent, doing their own thing. Maybe if Nate would agree to an arrangement like she and Pippa had, it could work. But she doubted he would. She also knew he'd want them to sleep together and she wasn't saying no about that. But marrying a man she wasn't in love with?

That wasn't something she was prepared to do.

When he didn't respond to her explanation of the difficulties in her parents' marriage, she raised another point. "Also, Hunter's wedding should really be the focus of the family right now. We don't want to steal any of the spotlight from him or Ferrin. Why don't we date? That's what you suggested earlier."

"Because when I suggested that, I had no idea that I had a daughter. I don't want to simply be dating a woman with a child. I want everyone to know she's mine," Nate said.

"I think you should tell everyone that you're her dad and then we can figure out us. I'm fine with dating or if you'd rather figure out the parenting thing first, we can wait," she said.

"You're saying that parent and partner are two different roles and I should just separate the two?"

he asked, moving a bit closer to her. She dropped her hands and eased subtly down the counter to put more distance between them.

The more she thought on this idea, the more she liked it. Nate had always been one of those guys she just couldn't resist, so it might be for the best if they kept things on a dating basis—at least until they got used to co-parenting Penny.

"I have a counterproposal for you," Nate said. He came closer to her, and she realized that his anger was gone now. In its place she noticed his steely-eyed determination to have things the way he wanted them.

"Go ahead."

"We try it your way. Tell Penny, and then our folks and my brothers, and explain that we are going to try living together to ease Penny's transition and give us a chance to get to know each other better."

She wasn't too sure she wanted to live with Nate. "I have a nanny, so I think we will be okay if you live in your house and I stay here."

"I don't think that," Nate said. "I want to meet the nanny and I'll decide if she can stay on—"

"No. You aren't coming in here and changing everything. We've been living our lives this way for a long time, and Pippa is the only person on the planet who has been with me from the beginning. I was alone in Vegas. Dad couldn't come out until after the baby was born, and when my water broke I was using public transportation and freaking out a little bit, but Pippa—a perfect stranger—helped me. She's not going anywhere," Kinley said.

It wasn't until she started talking that she realized how much she resented Nate for not being there for her. She'd thought she'd adjusted to everything. To having to do it all on her own. But hearing him say all the things he wanted…well, it ticked her off after she'd had to figure out so much of it by herself.

She blinked as she realized she was going to start crying. Dammit. She wasn't about to let him see her cry over something that she'd dealt with a long time ago. She blinked again, trying to keep the tears in her eyes, but she felt her nose and her cheeks heat up and knew they were probably bright red at this moment.

Nate walked toward her, and she put her arm up to keep him at a distance. "Don't."

He stopped, put his hands on his lean hips and looked at her, his blue-gray eyes filled with remorse and something else she couldn't read. "I'm sorry. I hadn't thought about what it was like for you to deal with a pregnancy on your own," he said at last. "I wish I'd been there for you."

"But you weren't," she said. She reached for the dish towel she'd left hanging on the handle of the stove and wiped her eyes with it. "I want us to figure out something that will be in everyone's best interest, but you must understand I'm not going to just blindly let you sweep in and make changes. I know that it isn't your way to let someone else take the lead, but in this case we are going to have to work together."

Nate nodded. "Fair enough."

Kinley took a deep breath. "You can spend some more time Penny tomorrow if you'd like, but I think you should go home now. I have a meeting in the morning, but it's with Ferrin so I might be able to postpone it. I'm not sure how your day is."

"I'll clear my schedule for you," Nate said. "I'm working out of the ranch office tomorrow. When you're done, bring Penny out to the ranch and we can tell her I'm her daddy and show her the horses and introduce her to her grandparents."

Kinley wasn't ready to face her dad and Nate's parents, but she had been mentally preparing herself for it after the cake tasting, when she'd seen the look on Ma Caruthers's face as she'd talked about grandchildren.

"Yeah, that sounds good," she said. She walked Nate to the door, but when they got there, he stopped her from opening it, pulling her into his arms and lowering his head to kiss her. When he lifted his mouth away from hers, he looked down into her eyes.

"Thank you for my daughter," he said, then turned and walked out into the night.

Twelve

Kinley texted Pippa that it was okay to come home and then went and climbed into Penny's bed, holding her daughter close as she slept. She didn't know what she'd expected would happen when she told Nate everything, but a part of her had expected to feel more relieved.

But to be honest, she felt more confused and conflicted than before. Talking about when she'd found out she was pregnant had brought back all of those emotions from when she'd been lonely and scared. She held Penny tighter and her daughter snuggled closer and Kinley let herself cry like she'd wanted to earlier in the kitchen.

It wasn't as if things were going to magically fix themselves. She was going to be in for some tough questions from her dad, and she wasn't sure how Ma Caruthers or Nate's father and brothers would react to her news.

A part of her wanted to pack her bags and Penny and leave. Just get in the car and pull a disappearing act like Pippa had. But the truth was that she couldn't do it. She'd never been one to run from trouble. She could take whatever they dished out to her.

She was used to fighting and being on the outside… *Oh, no.* That was it. What she truly feared was being alone again. When she had her secret about Penny, she'd been guaranteed to have her daughter with her. But now that Nate was back in the picture, everything was going to change—and she was very afraid of that.

She rolled onto her back, staring at the stars that Penny's night-light projected on the ceiling. When she was little sometimes her mom would climb into bed with her after a long night working in one of the houses and hold her. Kinley had always cherished those nights. Her entire life she'd been isolated a little by circumstances and by her nature.

She was very much afraid of trying to have a relationship with Nate, because none of hers really lasted. Sure, she had Pippa now, but once Pip decided to stop running and claim her real life, she'd leave.

And Pippa was different than Nate.

He was complicated and he made her feel things she wasn't sure she understood. Even when she was mad at him—and for a while when she'd been pregnant she'd tried to hate him—she couldn't stay mad. Even though she'd known it would have been smarter to stay away from him when she returned to Cole's Hill, she'd gone to dinner with him, slept with him.

And now…now she was going to have to figure out how to have a family with him. How to co-parent with a man who still intimidated her a little.

She kissed Penny's forehead and quietly let herself out of bed. She needed a plan. A real plan so she could manage herself and Nate. Otherwise she was going to find it hard to be strong tomorrow. And seeing Nate, his parents and her father was going to be difficult.

She had to be like Jacs. Tough but fair.

She would do it.

She was sitting on the couch working on her pro and con list when Pippa let herself in. She plopped down on the couch next to Kinley and gave her a sympathetic look. "How'd it go?"

"Awful. He wants us to get married," she said.

"What?"

"You heard that right. I said no. I mean, we hardly know each other."

"Didn't you sleep with him when you got here?" Pippa said, setting her purse on the coffee table and moving around on the couch until she was wedged into the corner and curling her legs up underneath her.

"I knew I shouldn't have told you about that," Kinley said. That was it. She couldn't resist him at times. He appealed to something inside her that felt wild and untamed. She didn't want to end up living her mom's life. She'd been miserable and hadn't really gotten any happier until they'd moved to California.

"You needed someone to talk to," Pippa said. "And I'm not bringing it up to be a bitch. I'm just saying you're not exactly immune to him."

Kinley groaned as she pulled her knees up to her chest and put her forehead on them. "What am I going to do?"

Pippa didn't even try to answer. No one could tell Kinley what to do in this situation.

She lifted her head. "The thing is, I don't regret telling him. You should have seen him with Penny tonight. I think he is going to be a way better dad than I ever would have suspected."

She scrambled to grab her phone from the coffee table and opened up the photo app and showed Pippa pictures from tonight. Of Nate helping Penny to decorate cookies, both of their heads bent over the cookie tray.

"Oh, Kinley, this is bad. He does look like he is going to be very involved in his daughter's life. Honestly, this is such a sweet picture...was this before you told him?"

Pippa handed her phone back, and Kinley took it and looked down at the screen. Nate was really an expert at being a good ol' boy and everybody's friend in Cole's Hill, but the expression on his face in this photo showed him as the real man. One who only let a few people in.

"Before," she said to Pippa.

She remembered the one other time she'd seen that softness in his expression. It had been their last morning together in Vegas, when the sun was creeping in and they were both trying to pretend that the weekend wasn't ending. That look had made her believe...

...in fairy tales.

But this was the real world, and she doubted tomorrow everyone in the Rockin' C kingdom was going to be excited to hear that she'd kept Penny a secret as long as she had.

But that wasn't what worried her the most. What worried her was her own soft heart and the fact that she might give in to Nate despite the fact she knew it would be a bad idea.

* * *

Nate drove straight from Kinley's house to the Rockin' C. As always when he drove onto the family land, he felt that sense of being where he belonged. The Texas summer sky looked huge illuminated by a full moon as he drove up the two-lane road that led past the bunkhouses and ranch family homes. He steered his own big inherited mansion and around onto a small, packed-dirt road that led to his parents' new place. He turned off the engine and coasted down into the driveway before putting the vehicle in Park and sitting there.

He wasn't about to wake his parents up at this time of night, but this had been the only place he'd thought to come. Now that he was here…what was he going to say to them?

He had a feeling they were going to be overjoyed about Penny but disappointed in him, and he couldn't really blame them. He was disappointed in himself.

Tonight he'd had a glimpse of something he had never realized he'd wanted. When his mom had said there was a solace in having a family that couldn't be explained, he always thought it was just her trying to get him and his brothers to settle down.

He'd never known that love for a child could completely overwhelm a person. Could completely overwhelm *him*.

He'd spent his entire life thinking he had it all and only tonight realized that something had been missing. Something he'd almost lost out on because he'd been too busy running around proving to everyone that he was the shit.

Except now he felt like shit. He should have known that Kinley might be pregnant. He should have listened to her instead of hanging up the phone the way he had.

He leaned forward and put his head on the steering wheel. How was it that he could handle troubled cattle, cantankerous business executives and rowdy rednecks, but one woman threw him into a tailspin?

There was a knock on the driver's door, and he turned to see his dad standing there with a flashlight.

Nate opened the door and stepped down onto the ground. "Hey, Dad."

"Son. You okay? Your mom thought she heard something and sent me out here to investigate... You know Derek showed up last night."

Nate hadn't known that. "Sorry for coming out here. I just didn't know where else to go."

"What's the matter?" his dad asked, walking back toward the house and the front porch.

Nate followed him up the steps and onto the porch toward the large rocking chairs that were waiting. His dad sat down in one and gestured for him to sit in the other. But Nate felt too restless to sit down. Instead he walked to the porch railing, put his hands on it and looked up at the moon.

"Son?"

"Sorry, Dad. It's just… I found out I have a kid tonight," he said.

"Congratulations," his dad said, clapping him on the shoulder. "How old is she or he? Who's the mom?"

His dad sounded so normal—too normal—that Nate turned to face him to see what he was thinking. This was the hardest part of all, he thought. How did he tell his dad this? He understood why Kinley had waited so long to tell him. It was a difficult thing to say. "I have a daughter, Dad. She's two, and Kinley Quinten is the mother."

"Marcus's daughter?" his dad asked. "Damn, boy, you know how to stir up a hornet's nest, don't ya?"

"Yes, sir," Nate said, coming over and sitting down next to his dad in a rocking chair. "Marcus doesn't know yet."

"Figured he didn't. He would have come after you with a shotgun," his dad said. "So I guess it'll have to be a double wedding."

Nate knew it. He was tempted to text Kinley and tell her to expect parental pressure tomorrow. But he didn't. "I'm not so sure. Kinley and I are still trying to figure that part out. For now, I've got a daughter, and I'm going to be a part of her life."

"Fair enough," his dad said. "But you know your mama isn't going to let you get away with waiting too long. You best get to winning that gal over."

For the first time since he'd found out he had a daughter, Nate felt some of the tension seep out of his neck. His dad made it sound so easy. Like there were steps he could take to make Kinley fall for him. If he knew the actions that would make that happen, she'd already be his.

But he didn't.

With her he was always operating on gut instinct and wild lust. Not the best combination to win. "How'd you do that with Mom?"

His father gave him a devilish smile and wriggled his eyebrows at him. "You're still not old enough to know those secrets, son. But I will say this—every woman has something she wants. Not gift-wise, but man-wise. You have to figure out what that thing is and show her you can deliver."

"Sex?" Nate asked.

"Hell, son, if it were that easy, you'd have been married ages ago."

"Funny, Dad, real funny."

"I know. You want me to tell your mom about your little girl... What's her name?"

"Penny. Well, Penelope Grace," Nate said, smiling when he remembered her hopping in and out of bed so many times. It felt like a million years ago instead of just a few hours. "No, I'll tell her. I think she'd rather hear it from me."

"Can't wait to meet her," his dad said.

"I feel like I've let you guys down," Nate said at last. "She's two."

"You haven't. We all make mistakes. The key is to fix them and move on. Don't let them define you."

Nate said good-night to his dad and drove home. He spent a restless night in bed thinking of how he was going to move forward as Penny's father and Kinley's man.

Kinley got out of bed at six o'clock after one of the worst nights of sleep she'd ever had. Penny woke up while Kinley was in the shower. Her daughter came in to talk to her, went potty and then headed back to Kinley's bedroom and climbed into Kinley's bed.

Standing under the shower spray, Kinley wondered how she was going to tell Penny about her father. She toweled off before putting on her robe and walking into the bedroom. Penny had turned the TV on and was lying at the foot of Kinley's bed watching her favorite show. She had her head propped up on her hands.

"Morning, sweet girl," Kinley said, sitting down next to her and giving her a kiss.

"Morning, Mama."

"So...you know how we talked about your daddy?"

Penny rolled over at her side and then sat up, crossing her legs underneath her little body. "Yeah."

"Well, he is ready to meet you," Kinley said. "How do you feel about that?"

"Yay. I want a daddy," Penny said, jumping up and then using the bounce from the bed to launch herself into Kinley's arms. She caught her easily and hugged her close.

"Good. You actually met him last night."

"The cowboy? My daddy is a cowboy?" Penny asked.

"Yes, he is."

"And he owns all those horsies," Penny said. "I am gonna have my own horsey."

Kinley had to laugh at the way her daughter said that. "Yes, you are. You have some other relatives, too. You're going to have some uncles, and your daddy has parents, so you'll have a grandma and a grandpa."

Penny stared at her, and Kinley wondered if she understood everything that she was being told. "Does Pippa know?"

"She does. And we are going to see your daddy after I go to work for a little while this morning."

"I have to go to school. It's my day to bring the snack," she said.

"I know. We can drop the snack off and then go meet your daddy. What do you think?"

Penny tipped her head to the side, pushing her long curls out of her face, and then nodded. "Okay, Mama."

Kinley finished getting dressed, answering questions that Penny came up with as she did. First she wanted to know where her daddy lived, and Kinley explained he lived on the same ranch as Pop-Pop, where they'd gone for the cookout. When Kinley was done putting on her clothes and makeup, they went to Penny's room to get her dressed. Penny wanted to look her best, so she wore a pair of cowboy boots, a pink skirt and her horse T-shirt.

She was squirmy while Kinley braided her hair and then raced to the kitchen, where Pippa was making breakfast, to tell her all she'd learned about her daddy.

Kinley was a little slower, texting Nate to see if he wanted to come to town and see Penny without his entire family and her father around. He texted back that he'd see her at the ranch house.

It was pretty abrupt, and she wondered if he was still mad at her. She suspected he was, and on some level she didn't blame him. But she thought they'd gotten closer to an understanding last night before he left.

"Pippa, can you take Penny to school to drop her snacks off and then bring her to my office around eleven? We are going to go out to the Rockin' C today."

"Yes, I can. Do you want me to come with you?"

"I think that would be a good idea. Someone is going to have to show Penny all those horses while I talk to everyone," Kinley said. She didn't want Penny to witness whatever the outcome was of telling the Carutherses and her dad about her and Nate. Her daughter was only two, so Kinley wasn't too sure how much adult conversation she'd understand, but she didn't want to chance it.

She poured her coffee into a to-go mug and gave her daughter a kiss before heading into her office. As soon as she was at her desk, she emailed Jacs and gave her a heads-up on what was going on. She didn't believe that Hunter would be so upset by the news that he'd fire her, but just in case, Kinley wanted her boss to be ready.

Then she picked up the phone to call her dad. She had no idea how she was going to ask him to meet with her without telling him why.

But she didn't want to tell him over the phone.

The call went to the answering machine. It really

was an old answering machine and not voice mail, because her dad didn't like newfangled gadgets.

"Hey, Dad, it's Kinley. I'm coming out to the Rockin' C later," she said. "I'm bringing Penny and I have something to talk to you about."

She hung up and then started looking through her wedding books and planning the happiest day for the brides she was working with. She wanted to pretend that her heart didn't ache just a little bit at the thought of her own love life, which was in the gutter as she planned perfect days for these other women.

Today it didn't seem as much fun as it always did, and maybe part of that was because Nate had offered to marry her not because he wanted to, but because he thought he should.

Never in the history of the world, she thought, had a woman ever wanted to be married to a man because he felt obligated. She knew this firsthand. She'd seen what that kind of marriage was like. As she told Nate last night, she'd grown up in a house where resentment and hatred had simmered between her parents.

And she didn't want that. But she looked down at the sketch of the dress that Ferrin had picked out and admitted to herself that she did want a husband of her own. It was just her bad luck that she had fallen for Nate again and he was the only man she could picture as her groom.

Thirteen

Nate was waiting for Kinley on the porch of the main ranch house when she pulled up. She got out of her car, wearing a short skirt and a fitted top. Another woman stepped out of the passenger side of the car. He'd seen her before, with Kinley and Penny at the coffee shop.

Kinley had her hair pulled up in one of those sophisticated updos that women seemed to love to wear. A pair of large sunglasses covered her face, and he wondered if she'd slept any better than he had the night before. She opened the back door of her car and stepped back so that Penny could get out. Their little girl hopped out of the car and then reached back inside to get a stuffed bunny and a brightly colored gift bag.

She saw him waiting for her and stopped in her tracks. The other woman called over to Kinley. "I'm going to wait over there. Holler when you need me."

Kinley gave the woman the thumbs-up sign, and Nate guessed she was the nanny.

Kinley crouched down to talk to Penny. They were too far away for him to hear what they were saying, but it seemed obvious to him that his daughter was afraid to come and meet him. So he went to her. He stooped down next to Kinley, and Penny turned to him.

"Penny, honey," he started but then realized he didn't know what to say. Blurting out that he was her father didn't seem the right thing, and just asking her if she knew also felt awkward to him. He touched the stuffed bunny under her arm with the lopsided lipstick marks on its mouth. "Who's this?"

"This is Mr. Beans," she said. "He wanted to come with me today to see my daddy."

"I'm glad he did," Nate said, holding his hand out to Mr. Beans. "It's very nice to meet you, Mr. Beans."

Penny set her bag down on the ground and then turned Mr. Beans so he could shake Nate's hand. Then she leaned in close to the stuffed bunny. "He is happy to meet you, too. We've been wantin' a daddy."

Nate scooped her into his arms and stood up, giving her a great big bear hug. She wrapped her little arms around his neck and hugged him back, and he realized that his life was never going to be the same again. He had a daughter.

Last night when he'd gotten the news, he hadn't thought of the long-term impact. The shock of learning he had a daughter had been enough to occupy him, but today, when he held her in his arms, he knew he never wanted to let her go.

He looked over at Kinley, who stood patiently watching them, and felt a little bit of resentment toward her that she'd had Penny all this time and he'd had nothing. Nothing but work, the ranch and temporary relationships. He knew that it had been his own choices that had given him that life, but he wanted something different now.

"Are you going to give me a lot of horsies?" Penny asked.

He shook his head. "No. I will probably give you a horse one day but you have to start learning to ride on a pony. Why is this bunny wearing lipstick?"

"He was feeling sad and needed cheering up," Penny said.

Nate turned toward his house as Kinley walked over to him. "I think we are going to need to talk about the horse. Penny can't have a horse in Nevada. My house is in a subdivision."

"I don't think that will be a problem," Nate said as they entered the house. "Since my daughter will be living with me."

"We still have to discuss where we are going to live. Penny, why don't you give your daddy the cookies we made for him, and then I'm going to get Pippa so you can play with her while we talk," Kinley suggested. She walked back to the front door and signaled her nanny.

"Thanks for the cookies," Nate said to Penny as he set her down.

"Nate, this is Pippa. Pippa, this is Nate," Kinley said as the other woman came into his home. "Where is a good place for them to hang out?"

"The game room is down the hall, second door on the right. There's a television and some board games and video games and a pool table."

"I think that will keep us busy," Pippa said in a crisp British accent that sort of surprised him.

But before he could ask her any questions, she'd taken Penny's hand and led her away. Nate turned to face Kinley and noticed she had a very stubborn look on her face.

"I have a list of things I think we should discuss," Kinley said. "First of all, don't make promises to Penny before we've had a chance to talk. She can't stay on the ranch with you, since our being in Texas is temporary."

He shook his head. "You've had too long being the only one who made decisions for our daughter. I'll make any promises I want to her. And your stay in Texas might be temporary, but Penny's isn't. She's my daughter and I want her here with me."

"Nate, be reasonable. She can't just start living here with you. She barely knows you. And my work is in town now, but I'll back in Vegas after Hunter's wedding."

"I think she'll know me well enough by the time you have to return to Nevada," he said. "Or you can reconsider my offer and stay here with me."

"No. It doesn't work that way. You gave up your rights when you hung up on me. You can get to know her now, but only because I'm letting you."

Kinley could tell already that today wasn't going to be a good one to talk to Nate. She didn't blame him for his anger, but she wasn't going to allow him to walk all over her, either. But she missed him and she wanted what she'd never had: Nate in her life, and not just for Penny. She didn't want to start off talking about how they'd co-parent like this. And it was even harder, because she'd sort of hoped that he'd have taken the night to realize that he wanted to be with her. That he'd say he wanted them to be a family. The three of them.

She wanted him to love her. Because she needed to know that he wanted her for herself and not just because they had a child together.

Instead he seemed set on telling her what to do.

"Letting me?" he echoed. "She's my daughter, too, Kinley. Don't forget that."

"I have never forgotten it, Nate. I can promise you that. Now, are you going to be reasonable?"

"Define reasonable," he said. "Because I think me having her on my own for two years would be a nice place to start."

Never. She would never give her daughter up, and she could see now that talking to him was getting her nowhere. She had an attorney that she'd visited in Nevada right after Penny was born who'd done the paperwork for her to leave the father's name blank on Penny's birth certificate. She also knew that Nate had no rights to Penny because he wasn't named as her father. But Kinley didn't want him to be cut out of Penny's life if he wanted to be part of it.

She took a deep breath. Nothing was going to be solved by being angry and fighting.

"I don't want either of us to be isolated from our daughter. Let's figure out a way that we can make this work," Kinley said. "I have already drawn up a list with a few ideas of ways we can try it out while I'm living here."

Nate took a deep breath and then turned away from her. "Let's discuss this in the den. Mrs. Haskins is around here somewhere, and I probably shouldn't have been yelling the way I was."

"You weren't that loud," Kinley said, following him into his den. It was decorated in very dark, masculine colors. The room was large and there were two guest chairs in front of a big mahogany desk. Bookcases lined the left wall, and the right wall had a big bay window that looked out over the pool. Behind his desk was a huge TV screen. He went around the desk and sat down, and she took a seat in one of the leather armchairs that had been provided for guests.

She set her bag on the floor by her feet and took out the notepad she'd jotted her thoughts on last night.

"To start with, I thought we could try letting her come out here during the day, and maybe on the weekends we could stay with Dad so you can see her," Kinley said.

"I want her to spend the night at my house," Nate said. "I'm her dad. How is she going to get to know me if she just visits?"

He had a point. But if Penny stayed here, then she'd have to as well. "I don't know if she'll spend the night away from me or Pippa. She's only ever stayed with the two of us."

"So you and Pippa can stay here with me. The house is big enough for the three of you to join me. Also, I want to decorate a room for her. Tell me what she likes and I'll get my decorator to start on it. I've already got her scheduled to come out here later in the week."

Kinley again felt like everything was spiraling out of her control; she wanted to run out of the room, grab Penny and drive far away from here. But she knew she couldn't. That it was too late for that. "Okay. I'm happy to work with your decorator, and Pippa is a great resource as well."

"I'll need Pippa's contact details," Nate said.

"Of course," Kinley said, but she wanted to talk to Pippa before she shared any information with Nate about her. She was on the run and only let a few people close enough to know her secret. "We should probably draw up some paperwork that has all of this spelled out."

"I'm not sure how we went from being lovers and starting to be friends to ending with paperwork to figure out how we'll raise our daughter. What is it you are so afraid of happening?"

Kinley sat back in the chair and had to force herself not to cross her arms over her chest. She didn't want to admit that trusting him was still hard for her. She didn't know if Nate was going to be there when things got real or if he'd flake out again.

"I'm not sure I trust you," she said at last.

"You can trust me," he said.

"I hope so. Because Penny deserves the best, and I'm not going to let you hurt her," Kinley said.

"Nice opinion you have of me," he said.

"Sorry. It's just been my experience."

"Three years ago," he said. "You're the one who left me the last time we slept together."

"I'm sorry about that. I just didn't know how to tell you about our daughter, and I didn't want to let myself believe that there could be something between us until you knew the truth."

"Do you still think there could be something between us?" he asked.

Yes. But she didn't want to say that or admit to feeling anything for him until she knew how he felt. He might be saying whatever he had to in order to get her to give up her rights to Penny.

She rubbed her forehead, feeling a headache coming on.

"Kinley?" he asked.

She licked her lips and looked over at him. Into those very serious blue-gray eyes that she knew she'd fallen in love with.

She started to tell him what he needed to hear. But what she wanted to say was that she wished there were something between them, because she was falling in love with him again.

But the door burst open behind them and her father was standing there with his shotgun in his left hand and his hat in the other.

"You son of a bitch, you better be prepared to do right by my daughter."

"Daddy! Stop it," Kinley said, jumping to her feet and rushing over to Marcus.

Nate stood up as well, feeling a heavy lump in the pit of his stomach. It wasn't only Penny and Kinley that Nate had to make up to for the last three years. He was going to have to make amends with Marcus and his own parents, too.

Marcus tossed his hat on the empty chair and then stood there with the shotgun held loosely in his arms. "Someone want to tell me what's going on? Babs only heard that you are Penny's father." Babs was the ranch's housekeeper.

"It was news to me as well," Nate said, putting his hands up. "There's no need for the gun. Why don't you put it down."

Marcus walked over to the sideboard under the window and set the gun on it and then turned back to face them both. The door opened again, and Nate groaned when she saw his parents standing there along with Derek and Hunter.

What the hell were they all doing here?

"Babs said that Marcus was headed over here with his gun, so we thought we'd better get over here, too," his father said.

"Dad, we don't need an audience right now."

"Why is Marcus here with his gun?" his mom asked.

Kinley stood up and cleared her throat. Everyone turned to look at her. She knotted her fingers together and then opened her mouth to speak, but no words came out.

She tried again. "Um...well, Nate and I have a daughter. But he's only just found out about her. Dad didn't know who the father was, either, and I think he's here to make sure that Nate does right by me. Which is silly, since it's the twenty-first century and I've been raising Penny on my own for two years."

"I have a granddaughter?" his mom asked. "Where is she? Can I see her?"

Kinley nodded. But Nate thought it was best to defuse this situation first. "Yes, Mom. To all of it. As soon as we get this sorted out, you can see her."

"What is there to sort out?" Marcus said. "You two getting married or not?"

"Your daughter just said she didn't want to marry me," Nate pointed out.

"That's not exactly true, but okay," Kinley said.

"Why didn't you tell Nate?" Marcus asked her.

"And why did you tell me that story about Penny's dad?"

Blushing, Kinley looked down at her shoes and then over at Nate. She hadn't told them anything about his behavior, and now she was trying to find some way to save him. To keep everyone in this room from knowing he was an ass.

He realized how much he loved her in that moment. And how much he didn't deserve her.

"It wasn't a story, Marcus," Nate said. "It happened just like she told you. She called me and I told her to get lost before she had a chance to tell me about her pregnancy."

Marcus made a grunt and exploded across the room, punching Nate in the jaw. For an older man, he packed a lot of power; the punch snapped Nate's head back and sent pain shooting through his jaw and down his neck.

His father ran toward Marcus, probably to stop him…or maybe to help him. And then Marcus's face convulsed. He grabbed at his chest and started to crumple right in front of Nate.

He reached for Kinley's dad as he started to fall, and Derek yelled for someone to call 911 as he rushed over from the doorway and started to do CPR.

"He's having a heart attack," Derek said. "Get the medevac out here."

Kinley was pale and shaking as she stood next to Nate and her father and waited for help to arrive. Nate put his arm around her, offering her some comfort. She patted his hand. Then clung to it. Even to Nate it felt as if time was moving in slow motion. He wasn't sure how long it was until Hunter came back in leading the EMTs.

"Can I go with you?" Kinley asked the medevac team.

"Only Dr. Caruthers. We don't have room for a passenger."

She nodded, and Nate grabbed his keys and put his hand under Kinley's elbow. "Come on. I'll drive you. Mom, Penny is in the game room with her nanny. Will you make sure they get to Cole's Hill?"

"Sure will, honey. You go with Kinley. I'll take care of our granddaughter."

"Are you sure, Ma Caruthers? I don't want to impose," Kinley said.

"Girl, you're family. There's no way you can impose. Now go on and make sure your daddy is all right."

Nate ushered Kinley into his truck, with Hunter in the backseat. Now and then, he looked over at Kinley nervously as they drove through town to the new medical facility on the outskirts of Cole's Hill. "Derek is one of the best cardiologists in the state. You know that he will save your dad."

Even as Nate said that, he remembered the other night and how Derek had lost a patient but told himself that was the exception. Derek was one of the top-rated cardiologists in the country and he would do everything in his power to save Marcus.

Kinley was white as a ghost as he pulled up in front of the medical center. He put the truck in Park and Kinley hopped out of the vehicle, heading toward the front door. He followed her, knowing that Hunter would park the truck for him.

When Nate caught up with her, Kinley was at the desk trying to get some information, looking very small and very alone. He came over to her and put his arm around her and then signaled for a nurse to come and help them. Kinley looked up at him, almost surprised that he was still here, and he realized that this was how she'd been for the last three years—on her own and having to deal with everything. She didn't know how to lean on someone, because no one had been there for her. But now he was here.

Fourteen

The hospital where Derek performed the emergency operation on Kinley's father was on the outskirts of Cole's Hill in a new medical park that had opened five years ago. She'd been sleeping in her dad's room since he'd come out of surgery two days ago. She hovered over him, seeing to the oxygen tube in his nose, watching his pale face for any signs of trouble as he slept.

The only way he could sleep was when the nurses gave him sleeping pills. They hadn't had a chance to talk about anything since his heart attack. She felt guilty; maybe learning that Nate was Penny's father had brought it on, though Derek had been pretty clear that her dad's arteries had been in bad shape for a while. If she was grateful for anything, it was that Derek had been at the Rockin' C when her dad had the heart attack.

She still replayed in her mind the moment when he'd started to collapse and she ran toward him. She'd never get over seeing him like that.

Her dad.

The biggest, strongest, toughest cowboy she knew, crumpling to the ground as they all stared on in shock. Derek had been the first to know what was happening.

"Kinley?"

"I'm here, Daddy," she said. "What do you need?"

"Some water would be nice," he said. "I'd get it for myself, but I'm too damned weak."

"I don't mind doing it for you," she said. "That's why I'm here." Kinley poured him some water from the pitcher on the nightstand and then adjusted his bed, being careful of the IV in his arm as she did so. His left arm was completely black-and-blue, and just seeing it made tears sting her eyes. She blinked them back as she handed him his cup of water.

He took it from her, his hand shaking as he tried to lift it to his mouth. She put her hand under his and helped to steady it as he drank. He didn't say anything to her as he let go of the cup and she put it back on the table.

She leaned over him and hugged him carefully. With his free arm, he hugged her back.

"I'm sorry if hearing about me and Nate shocked you," Kinley said at last.

"It did, but that's not what caused this. Derek has been after me for the last six months to cut back on my salt," Marcus said. "I was surprised you didn't say anything about Nate earlier."

She paused and searched for the right words to tell him how embarrassed she'd felt and how she knew if she'd told him about Nate it would make things awkward for him. He loved the Rockin' C. It was his home. She'd never wanted to jeopardize that.

She nibbled on her lower lip. "I wanted to, but I knew that it would put you in an awkward situation."

"So instead you isolated yourself," he said. "Do you know how that makes me feel?"

"Pretty awful, I'd guess," she said. "But that might be the effect of your heart attack." She hoped he'd smile, and he did manage a weak one.

"It might be," he admitted. "You look tired. Why don't you go home and get some rest?"

"I don't want you to be alone." And she'd never say this out loud to him, but she was afraid to leave him. Her dad was the only parent she had left, and his heart attack had scared her and made he realize how much she still needed him.

"He won't be."

Kinley turned to see Ma Caruthers and her husband, Brody, standing there in the doorway. "We will keep an eye on him while you go rest."

Kinley looked at her dad and he nodded. She walked over toward Nate's parents, a million words that she hadn't had a chance to say swirling around in her head. She hoped they didn't hate her, but wouldn't blame them if they did. But instead of saying anything to her, Ma Caruthers pulled her close and hugged her. And then Brody clapped a hand on her shoulders.

"You have to take care of yourself as well," he said.

"Thank you," she said to them both. They were nice people, and with everything that had happened in the last few days and her lack of sleep, Kinley knew she was on the edge of crying again. She tried to keep it together, blinking like crazy.

"Call me if anything happens with Dad. I'll be back in a few hours," she said and walked away before she lost it completely.

When she got out to the parking lot, she couldn't remember what her car looked like and just stood there staring at the vehicles, waiting and hoping she'd remember.

A black pickup truck pulled up in front of her, and Nate leaned over to open the passenger door. "Want a ride home?"

She did. But she remembered the fight they'd had in front of his family, and she wasn't too sure leaning on him and taking a ride from him was the best idea.

"Nate—"

"Don't worry about anything. Your dad just had a heart attack and you're tired. I'd have to really be a bastard to be anything but a friend to you right now."

She nodded and climbed up into the cab of the truck. Putting on her seat belt, she realized that everyone was being very nice to her. And for the first time since her mom had died, she truly felt like she was part of a family.

"Thank you."

"You're welcome. I hope you don't mind, but I told Penny I was coming to get you."

"I don't mind," Kinley said.

When they got to her house, Penny stood in the doorway wearing the horse shirt that her grandfather had given her, jeans, her cowboy boots and a pair of fairy wings.

"Where did the wings come from?"

"She heard my mom say that your dad needed

lots of angels around him and wanted her own wings, so I got her some," Nate said.

Kinley nodded her thanks to Nate and got out of the truck as Penny ran down the walk toward her. She scooped her little girl up and held her close, finally letting the tears that had been threatening fall.

"Your pop-pop is okay," Kinley told her. "We're going to go visit him after I get some sleep."

Nate waited until Kinley was sleeping before he checked his phone. He had a text from Ethan telling him he needed to stop by the office.

Pippa was in the kitchen with Penny, who was decorating heart-shaped cookies for Marcus.

"Hi, Daddy," Penny said.

She'd been calling him Daddy every time she saw him. And it warmed his heart to see how happy she was to have him in her life. He wished he'd handled things with Kinley better, but his temper had always had gotten the best of him and he'd reacted without thinking things through.

Now he had to figure out how to make it all up to her. "Hi, angel. How are the cookies coming along?"

"Good. Pippa is already baking them."

"That's right, and then we'll frost them," Pippa said.

Nate came over to the breakfast table where Penny was sitting and dropped a kiss on the top of her head. "I have to run over to my office to do some work. Will you be okay with Pippa until I get back?"

"Yes, Daddy."

"Pippa, is that okay?"

"Sure is," she said.

"Good. I'll be back in an hour. If Kinley wakes and needs anything, let me know," he said.

By the time he got finished with his meetings, it was nearly three in the afternoon. The board was discussing fracking for shale oil on their property. Oil was one of their income streams, and Nate knew that many members of the board wanted to try to diversify. But he wasn't satisfied yet that fracking was the way forward. They agreed to table the issue for now. He adjourned the board meeting and then went into his office to finish up some paperwork so he could have the next few days free to help Kinley and her dad with whatever they needed.

He'd already arranged to have an in-home nurse stay with Marcus until he was fully recovered. Once Nate talked with Kinley, he'd figure out if she wanted her father to stay in town with her or if the nurse would stay with Marcus at his house on the ranch.

"You have a call on line one," Nate's assistant called from the outer office.

He lifted the handset. "This is Caruthers."

"Nate, it's Ethan. How's Marcus doing? Is he okay?"

Nate rubbed the back of his neck, tucking the phone between his neck and shoulder. "Yeah, Derek thinks he's going to make a full recovery, but it will take some time for him to be back to normal."

"Thank God. I'm heading toward the airport now. I'll be back on the ranch tonight. I wanted to talk to you about your daughter. I started working on the papers you requested for custody—"

"I've changed my mind. Obviously we can share custody, as long as Kinley will agree to it," Nate said. He knew that he'd felt backed into a corner when he'd made the decision to sue for full custody.

He'd been angry and disappointed by all he'd missed out when he'd thought about suing for full custody but even as he'd pursued that by asking Ethan to look into it, he knew he'd never go through it. Penny and Kinley belonged together. A part of him had been worried he wouldn't fit in.

And if he were being brutally honest, he wanted to hurt Kinley a little. But that had been anger and not the rational man he was.

Part of it had been because of the disappointment on his mom's face, and the other part had been guilt and anger at himself for not being the better man. He'd thought if he had full custody he could make up for that... Hell, he'd wanted to hurt Kinley, too.

But Marcus's heart attack had taken the teeth out of Nate's anger, and he'd realized that when it came to family, there wasn't any reason to be selfish. Penny was his, and Kinley hadn't denied that. They'd figure out something that worked for them without involving lawyers.

"I'm glad to hear that. I would have done what you wanted, but the whole intent of this call was to talk you out of it," Ethan said. "I'm pretty sure you would regret taking Kinley to court. If we won, things would always be weird between you, and I think that would affect your daughter."

"You're right," Nate said to his brother. "I have an idea and I could use your help with it."

"Whatever you need," Ethan said.

Nate described what he hoped Ethan would do for him. And Ethan laughed as he heard Nate's plan but just said he'd do it. After he hung up the phone with Ethan, Nate called Derek and got an update on Marcus's condition.

"He's doing good, Nate. One of the best things was that the air ambulance was nearby, thanks to the NASA facility, and they were able to get us to the hospital so quickly. The surgery went well and when I was him a few minutes ago he looked good. Well, aggravated but also pretty good," Derek said.

"Why was he aggravated?" Nate asked. He knew

he still needed to make his peace with Marcus now that the other man knew he was Penny's father.

"He didn't like it when I told him it was going to be at least six months before I cleared him to go back to work," Derek said.

"That sounds like Marcus," Nate said. "Did the news about me and Kinley affect him? Did it bring on his heart attack?"

"Not at all. This was a long time in the making," Derek said.

Nate wanted to believe his brother, but he had seen how purple Marcus's face had gotten when he'd punched him, and Nate was not going to be able to forgive himself for putting Marcus in that position for a long time.

He drove back to Kinley's house and arrived just as Kinley and Penny were getting ready to go visit Marcus. He offered them a ride, but Kinley declined, saying she would drive herself.

He wanted to argue with her, but he'd done enough of that for this week and instead simply followed her to the hospital in his own truck.

When they got to the hospital, Penny ran to Nate as soon as he got out of his truck and he scooped her up. It was hard seeing Penny run to him the way she did, and Kinley realized that her daughter had missed having a father. She wished she'd found a way to tell him sooner. Things had gotten so out of hand between them, and then her dad had punched him…

"I don't know if they are going to let Penny in to see Dad," Kinley said, walking over to them. "If they don't—"

"I'll keep her with me. Where's Pippa?"

"She's going to pick Jacs up at the airport," Kinley said. Her boss had insisted on flying out to Texas and taking over all of Kinley's appointments for the next week to give Kinley time with her father.

"Who is Jacs?" Nate asked, shifting Penny to his other arm so he could reach out and hold open the hospital door for her. She walked in front of him and then stopped inside, taking off her sunglasses.

Nate was wearing suit pants, a dress shirt and tie. He looked every inch the CEO today, but then she noticed his cowboy boots and realized he hadn't left the ranch behind.

"My boss," Kinley said. It was funny to her that Nate knew so much about her but not something as simple as her boss's name. There were a lot of things to work out, she realized. She and Nate needed to sit down and talk.

"We really need some time to discuss Penny and the future," she said. After the way the entire Caruthers family had rallied around her and her dad, she knew that she wanted to be a part of the family, and she was hoping that maybe Nate would feel the same way.

"Of course. But let's sort out your dad first," Nate said.

She nodded. Dad was everyone's top priority. She led the way down the hall to her father's room, but when they got to the nurses' station, they hesitated.

"Is it okay if my daughter comes in to see her grandfather?" Kinley asked.

"It sure is," the nurse said. "Dr. Caruthers already cleared her for a visit."

"Thanks," Nate said.

Kinley finished leading them down the hall, and Nate set Penny on her feet. "Go in and visit with your pop-pop. I'll be right out here."

Kinley opened the door for Penny and then looked back at Nate. "Why aren't you coming in?"

"The last time he saw me, he threw a punch. I'm not sure your dad is going to want to see me again so soon."

"I'll let you know," Kinley said. Remorse was a tough thing to live with, and Kinley was feeling it in spades today. She'd come between her father and Nate. She'd come between her daughter and Nate, and she was pretty sure she'd ruined any chance she and Nate had for a future together that didn't involve just parenting their daughter.

And that hurt more than she expected it to.

"Hi, Pop-Pop," Penny said, running toward his bed.

Kinley hurried after her, catching her and lifting her up before she reached the bed. She didn't want to take a chance on Penny pulling on any of the IVs.

"Hi, there. Is that my granddaughter or a little angel?" Marcus asked, holding out his arms for Penny.

Kinley carefully set her daughter on his lap. "Watch out for these tubes, Penny."

"I will," she said as Marcus snuggled her close to him with the arm that wasn't attached to the IV. "I'm an angel, Pop-Pop. Grandma said you needed them."

"I do need them," he said to Penny.

Penny continued doing what she did best—talking and laughing—and Kinley noticed that her father seemed more relaxed with Penny in his arms. Now she had another regret to add to the many that she'd been carrying with her today—that she'd limited them to a relationship conducted by video chat instead of one that was in person.

Derek came into the room with an orderly. "How are you feeling today, Marcus?"

"Better than I did yesterday," her father answered.

"Good to hear it," Derek said.

Derek asked Marcus a bunch of questions about how he was feeling and made some notes in his file. "I want to check your heart."

Marcus lifted Penny up, and Derek took her and set her on her feet next to him. Kinley came and got her and they both stood over near the guest chair while Derek finished checking her father out. "My office manager will be calling you to set up an appointment. It's important that you don't miss any of the pills I've prescribed. Nate has arranged for an in-home nurse, and he asked me to recommend a few. Two of the candidates will be by later and a third tomorrow morning. It's going to take you months to recover, Marcus, so make sure you select the nurse you think you can work with for that long."

"I don't need a nurse," Marcus said. "I'll be fine on my own."

"Don't be stubborn, Dad. He's going to stay with me in town—"

"He's sitting right here, daughter. I'll stay at my own place. You have enough to worry about with Penny," Marcus said.

Kinley took a deep breath and realized just how hardheaded her father could be. "We haven't decided anything yet."

"Fair enough," Derek interjected. "Colin is here to take you for some blood work."

"Can I go with him?" Penny asked.

Derek looked at her and then stooped down to Penny's level. "You can push him down the hall to the elevator with me, and then I'll bring you back to your mom. How's that sound?"

"Perfect."

Kinley stepped into the hallway and watched as her little angel pushed her grandfather down to the elevator. Then she glanced up and saw Nate waiting there, and she knew it was time to sort out her future. And she hoped that there would be one with this man.

Fifteen

Nate went by the hospital the next evening when he knew that Kinley, Penny and his parents were all having dinner together. He wanted a chance to talk to Marcus, to make things right.

He knocked on the hospital room door and stuck his head in before entering. "Do you mind if I come in?"

Marcus was sitting in bed watching PBR on the television. He muted the TV before motioning for Nate to come in. Nate closed the door behind himself and walked over to the bed. He knew that Marcus was recovering well from his heart attack; Nate had seen him a few times through the door, but it did him good to see the older man sitting up in bed after the last time he'd seen him crumpling in front of him.

"What's up, son?" Marcus said.

Marcus's kind tone humbled him and made him realize that he had been right to wait and come and talk to him alone. "I wanted to apologize, sir."

"Kinley already explained things," Marcus said.

"She did?"

"Yes. But you and I both know that girl is sweet on you, so I'm not buying half of what she said," Marcus explained. "I think it did happen the way she originally said, and I'm pretty sure you're not in the same frame of mind you were three years ago when she got pregnant."

"You're correct, sir. I want to make it up to her. Figure out a way to show her that I have changed and that she doesn't have to be on her own anymore."

Marcus nodded, crossing his arms over his chest as he leaned back against the pillows. "That might not be easy. She might like you, but…her mom and I married because of Kinley, and Rita never really forgave me for it. She and I were never meant to be together forever and neither of us really tried. Our folks said we should marry, so we did."

Nate remembered how he felt when Marcus had burst into his den with the shotgun and could understand why that wouldn't be the best start to a marriage. But he wanted to spend the rest of his life with Kinley, and he wanted Penny to have some siblings, too. So Nate knew he was going to have to figure out how to change her mind. Figure out how to show her that he was the kind of man she could count on.

"I'm not going anywhere, and I'll wait as long as it takes for her to see that I'm serious about her. I want your permission to ask her to marry me," Nate said. He knew Kinley would take some convincing, but he wanted to make sure that Marcus understood that he did respect him despite the behavior that had led to this situation.

"You have it, son, but I don't think it's going to be easy to convince her to say yes."

Nate didn't, either. Which was why he was starting with the tough guy in the hospital. Marcus was daunting, but Kinley was doubly so, and Nate was only starting to realize just how tough and self-reliant she was.

"You're not exactly telling me news I don't know," Nate said. "But I have a plan."

"Good. You're going to need one. And you might need a few allies," Marcus said.

Nate already had his brother helping him set up everything so that it was just right, and it had taken a lot of talking but eventually he'd gotten Pippa on board to help him out, too. He would have gone to Penny, but it seemed like cheating to use their daughter so he'd ask Pippa to just tell her they had a surprise for Kinley, and he didn't want Kinley to feel trapped. He wanted her to only say yes when she was convinced that he was the man she wanted by her side for the rest of her life.

He stayed with Marcus for another hour, talking to him about ranch business and reassuring him that his job would be waiting for him when he returned. "It's not like anyone else can do you job."

"Damned straight. No one knows that place like me. Except maybe your dad, but he's retired now," Marcus said.

Nate was thinking it might be time for Marcus to retire, too, but Derek had recommended putting off talking about that until he was fully recovered. Derek said state of mind made a huge difference in the speed of recovery, and men who thought they had someone waiting for them recovered quicker.

"My dad's not really that retired. He still shows up unannounced at my office in town when he feels like it. I'm hoping that Penny will take up some of his time. Can you believe that Kinley hasn't had her on a horse yet?"

"It's a sin. I was thinking we could start Penny out on Abigail. She's such a sweet mare. She'd be perfect, and you could ride double with her until she gets used to being up there on the horse."

Nate had been thinking along the same lines. "I'll do it until Derek gives you the okay to ride again. You're a genius with horses, so maybe she'll pick up some of your skills."

"Deal," Marcus said.

Nate checked his watch and realized he needed to get moving so that he was at the ranch when Kinley got there. He had talked Pippa into bringing her out to pick up some stuff for Marcus.

Twenty minutes after saying his goodbyes to Kinley's dad, Nate pulled up to the barn at the Rockin' C and parked his truck. He walked into the barn to see if everything was set up and was pleased to discover that Ethan had taken care of every detail just as he'd requested.

Penny and Pippa were up to something. She could tell by the way Penny kept trying to wink at Pippa when she thought Kinley wasn't looking. Her daughter couldn't really wink; she closed both eyes and then opened one up with her fingers instead. It was one of the most adorable things Kinley had ever seen.

As soon as Pippa said they needed to go to the Rockin' C, she suspected that whatever they were up to involved Nate. She was happy enough to go along with it, since she had missed Nate. He'd been very sweet since her dad's heart attack.

In a bunch of different, quiet ways he'd made her feel that she wasn't on her own when it came to dealing with her father's heart attack and the aftermath.

The live-in nurse he'd hired for them was very nice and efficient and seemed charmed by her father's gruff manner. Nate had also offered his penthouse apartment to Jacs for her to stay in while she was in town. When he'd realized that Pippa didn't drive, he assigned the task to one of his ranch hands so she had her own driver.

And of course Kinley couldn't really forget that moment before her father had burst into the den, when something had passed between the two of them and she'd almost told him she loved him.

Pippa directed her to park in front of her father's house, which was located adjacent to the barn.

"Penny and I will go and gather some of Marcus's things. He wanted you to check on his favorite horse. Take as long as you like. We've got things to do, right, imp?"

"That's right. Take as long as you want," Penny said, then blew Kinley a kiss as she got out of the car.

Kinley waited until they were both inside her dad's house before walking to the barn. As soon as she got close, she noticed that there were lights on inside, and she heard the sound of music.

When she opened the barn door, she saw that twinkle lights had been draped over the beams and a table and chair sat in the middle of the main aisle. On the table was an old-fashioned telephone. She walked farther into the room and looked down at the tabletop.

But there was no note.

The phone started ringing, which she thought was odd, since it wasn't attached to the wall. But she answered it.

"Hello, Kinley," Nate said. His voice was deep and husky. She smiled to herself as she sat down in the chair next to the table.

"Hello, Nate," she said.

"I know we said that everything between us would just be for one weekend," he started.

She swallowed the lump in her throat as she realized he was using the exact words she had when she'd called him almost three years ago.

"We did say that."

"But circumstances have changed. I know that I said what happens in Vegas stays there, but do you know what happens in Cole's Hill?"

She shook her head and then wondered if he could see her.

"No, I don't."

"Well, what happens in Cole's Hill is forever, and I'm not sure how you feel after the way our last call ended, but I want to spend the rest of my life with you," he said. Now she heard him next to her, not through the phone. She turned to see him standing there.

He held a ring box in one hand. She put the phone back on the table and turned to face him. "I know I haven't made things easy for us, but I love you, Kinley. And I want to spend the rest of my life with you. Not because we have a beautiful daughter, though I want her, too. But because you are you, and my life will not be complete without you."

He went down on one knee and held the ring box out to her. "Will you marry me?"

"Are you sure you are doing this because you want to marry me and not because you think you have to?"

"Kin, have you ever known me to do anything because I have to?"

"No. Is it because my dad had a heart attack?"

"Not at all. Though you should know I asked him for his permission to marry you, and he gave it to me."

She chewed her lower lip. *Yes* hovered on her lips. She loved him and wanted to marry him. It was the secret she'd kept closer to her heart than Penny's dad.

"I need to make this right for us, because when you and I are sixty and our grandkids ask us how we fell in love, I want them to know that I fell for you so hard that I couldn't imagine living another day without you."

"Me, either," she said. "I love you, too, Nate. And I will marry you."

Nate let out a whoop and lifted her out of the chair and swung her around in a circle. He held her tightly to him as he kissed her.

He put her on her feet and took the engagement ring and put it on her finger. She looked down at it. It was simple and elegant and absolutely perfect.

Kinley remembered how afraid she'd been to come back to Cole's Hill, but now she was glad she had come. She had been afraid of the unknown and of facing Nate again, but together they were going to have a wonderful future together.

"We have to tell Penny…unless you already did?"

He shook his head. "Not a chance. I had to ask you before I started telling anyone else."

"I love you, Nate Caruthers."

"Not as much I love you, Kinley soon-to-be-Caruthers."

He pulled her into his arms and kissed her. Finally it felt like coming home. Like the place that she'd been searching for was really a person. Nate. It was hard to believe it after all they'd been through and how she'd almost given up on him…*had* given up on him.

But now he was holding her as if he'd never let

go and looking down at her with love in his eyes and she knew deep in her soul that this was what she'd been missing.

Being a mom had satisfied something inside of her but being in Nate's arms, knowing he was going to spend the rest of his life with her made her realize this was what she'd secretly wanted all along.

They told Penny, who was very happy. Pippa also congratulated them. Then they drove back to Marcus's hospital room, and all of the family gathered there to hear the news. Kinley, who had felt alone for so long, had the family she'd always dreamed of and the only man she'd ever loved by her side.

* * * * *

Don't miss any of these sweet and sexy reads from USA TODAY *bestselling author Katherine Garbera.*

HIS BABY AGENDA
HIS SEDUCTION GAME PLAN
HIS INSTANT HEIR
BOUND BY A CHILD
FOR HER SON'S SAKE

Available now from Harlequin Desire!
***
If you're on Twitter, tell us what you think
of Harlequin Desire! #harlequindesire.

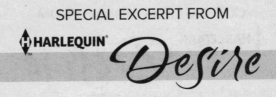
*When billionaire boss Cameron McNeill goes
undercover in a tropical paradise to check out his
newest hotel's employees, he doesn't expect to want to
claim beautiful concierge Maresa Delphine and her
surprise baby as his own...*

*Read on for a sneak peek at
HIS ACCIDENTAL HEIR
by Joanne Rock*

As soon as he banished the hotel staff, including Maresa
Delphine, he'd find a quiet spot on the beach where he
could recharge.

Maresa punched a button on the guest elevator while
a young man disappeared down another hall with the
luggage. Cameron's gaze settled on the bare arch of her
neck just above her jacket collar. Her thick brown hair
had been clipped at the nape, ending in a silky tail that
curled along one shoulder. A single pearl drop earring
was a pale contrast to the rich brown of her skin.

She glanced up at him. Caught him staring.

The jolt of awareness flared hot and unmistakable. He
could tell she felt it, too. Her pupils dilated a fraction,
dark pools with golden rims. His heartbeat slugged
heavier. Harder.

He forced his gaze away as the elevator chimed to
announce their arrival on his floor. "After you."

He held the door as she stepped out into the short hall. Cameron used the key card to unlock the suite, not sure what to expect. So far, Maresa had proven a worthy concierge. That was good for the hotel. Less favorable for him, perhaps, since her high standards surely precluded acting on a fleeting elevator attraction.

"If everything is to your satisfaction, Mr. Holmes, I'll leave you undisturbed while I go make your dinner reservations for the week." She hadn't even allowed the door to close behind them, a wise practice, of course, for a female hotel employee.

The young man he'd seen earlier was already in the hall behind her with the luggage cart. Cameron could hear her giving the bellhop instructions.

"Thank you." Cameron turned his back on her to stare out at the view of the hotel's private beach and the brilliant turquoise Caribbean Sea. "For now, I'm satisfied."

The room, of course, was fine. Ms. Delphine had passed his first test.

But satisfied? No.

He wouldn't rest until he knew why the guest reviews of the Carib Grand Hotel were less positive than anticipated. And satisfaction was the last thing he was feeling when the most enticing woman he'd met in a long time was off-limits.

That attraction would be difficult to ignore when it was imperative he uncover all her secrets.

Don't miss
HIS ACCIDENTAL HEIR by Joanne Rock,
available June 2017 wherever
Harlequin® Desire books and ebooks are sold.

www.Harlequin.com

HARLEQUIN
Desire

AVAILABLE JUNE 2017

A TEXAS-SIZED SECRET

BY *USA TODAY* BESTSELLING AUTHOR

MAUREEN CHILD,

PART OF THE SIZZLING
TEXAS CATTLEMAN'S CLUB: BLACKMAIL SERIES.

When Naomi finds herself pregnant and facing scandal, her best friend steps up. He claims the baby as his own and offers to marry her, in name only. But his solution leads to a new problem—she might be falling for him!

AND DON'T MISS A SINGLE INSTALLMENT OF

BLACKMAIL

No secret—or heart—is safe in Royal, Texas...

The Tycoon's Secret Child
by *USA TODAY* bestselling author Maureen Child

Two-Week Texas Seduction by Cat Schield

Reunited with the Rancher
by *USA TODAY* bestselling author Sara Orwig

Expecting the Billionaire's Baby by Andrea Laurence

Triplets for the Texan
by *USA TODAY* bestselling author Janice Maynard

A Texas-Sized Secret
by *USA TODAY* bestselling author Maureen Child

AND

July 2017: *Lone Star Baby Scandal* by Golden Heart® Award winner Lauren Canan
August 2017: *Tempted by the Wrong Twin* by *USA TODAY* bestselling author Rachel Bailey
September 2017: *Taking Home the Tycoon* by *USA TODAY* bestselling author Catherine Mann
October 2017: *Billionaire's Baby Bind* by *USA TODAY* bestselling author Katherine Garbera
November 2017: *The Texan Takes a Wife* by *USA TODAY* bestselling author Charlene Sands
December 2017: *Best Man Under the Mistletoe* by *USA TODAY* bestselling author Kathie DeNosky

Whatever You're Into… Passionate Reads

Looking for more passionate reads from Harlequin®?
Fear not! Harlequin® Presents, Harlequin® Desire and
Harlequin® Blaze offer you irresistible romance stories
featuring powerful heroes.

♥HARLEQUIN *Presents*.

Do you want alpha males, decadent glamour and jet-set
lifestyles? Step into the sensational, sophisticated world of
Harlequin® Presents, where sinfully tempting heroes ignite a
fierce and wickedly irresistible passion!

♥HARLEQUIN *Desire*

Harlequin® Desire novels are powerful, passionate and
provocative contemporary romances set against a backdrop of
wealth, privilege and sweeping family saga. Alpha heroes with
a soft side meet strong-willed but vulnerable heroines amid a
dramatic world of divided loyalties, high-stakes conflict and
intense emotion.

♥HARLEQUIN *Blaze*.

Harlequin® Blaze stories sizzle with strong heroines and
irresistible heroes playing the game of modern love and lust.
They're fun, sexy and always steamy.

Be sure to check out our full selection of books
within each series every month!

www.Harlequin.com

HPASSION2016

Get 2 Free Books,

HARLEQUIN *Desire*

Plus 2 Free Gifts —

just for trying the *Reader Service!*

HDI7